A KISS IN T.

They were some distance away from the house when there was the sound of a gunshot followed by several others.

The Sheik turned his horse round to look back and there appeared to be some commotion in front of his house.

From the distance Vanda could not see what was happening.

A number of tribesmen started to ride towards the turmoil and there must have been a dozen or more men in front of her riding towards the house.

She was suddenly aware that two horses had closed in beside hers.

She looked at them.

They were ridden by men who seemed at first glance to be differently dressed from any of the tribesmen she had seen so far.

She was just about to speak to them hoping they would understand her, when to her astonishment they seized the reins of her mare and without a word they started to lead her swiftly away into the desert.

"What are you doing? What is happening?" Vanda demanded.

Even as she spoke the two men on either side of her quickened their horses and started to gallop, pulling her horse with them.

"Stop! Who are you? Where are you going?"

THE BARBARA CARTLAND PINK COLLECTION

Titles in this series

1. The Cross of Love
2. Love in the Highlands
3. Love Finds the Way
4. The Castle of Love
5. Love is Triumphant
6. Stars in the Sky
7. The Ship of Love
8. A Dangerous Disguise
9. Love Became Theirs
10. Love Drives In
11. Sailing to Love
12. The Star of Love
13. Music is the Soul of Love
14. Love in the East
15. Theirs to Eternity
16. A Paradise on Earth
17. Love Wins in Berlin
18. In Search of Love
19. Love Rescues Rosanna
20. A Heart in Heaven
21. The House of Happiness
22. Royalty Defeated by Love
23. The White Witch
24. They Sought Love
25. Love is the Reason for Living
26. They Found Their Way to Heaven
27. Learning to Love
28. Journey to Happiness
29. A Kiss in the Desert

A KISS IN THE DESERT

BARBARA CARTLAND

.com

Barbaracartland.com Ltd

THE BARBARA CARTLAND PINK COLLECTION

Barbara Cartland was the most prolific bestselling author in the history of the world. She was frequently in the Guinness Book of Records for writing more books in a year than any other living author. In fact her most amazing literary feat was when her publishers asked for more Barbara Cartland romances, she doubled her output from 10 books a year to over 20 books a year, when she was 77.

She went on writing continuously at this rate for 20 years and wrote her last book at the age of 97, thus completing 400 books between the ages of 77 and 97.

Her publishers finally could not keep up with this phenomenal output, so at her death she left 160 unpublished manuscripts, something again that no other author has ever achieved.

Now the exciting news is that these 160 original unpublished Barbara Cartland books are ready for publication and they will be published by Barbaracartland.com exclusively on the internet, as the web is the best possible way to reach so many Barbara Cartland readers around the world.

The 160 books will be published monthly and will be numbered in sequence.

The series is called the Pink Collection as a tribute to Barbara Cartland whose favourite colour was pink and it became very much her trademark over the years.

The Barbara Cartland Pink Collection is published only on the internet. Log on to www.barbaracartland.com to find out how you can purchase the books monthly as they are published, and take out a subscription that will ensure that all subsequent editions are delivered to you by mail order to your home.

If you do not have access to a computer you can write for information about the Pink Collection to the following address :

Barbara Cartland.com Ltd.
Camfield Place,
Hatfield,
Hertfordshire AL9 6JE
United Kingdom.

Telephone : +44 (0)1707 642629
Fax :   +44 (0)1707 663041

THE LATE DAME BARBARA CARTLAND

Barbara Cartland who sadly died in May 2000 at the age of nearly 99 was the world's most famous romantic novelist who wrote 723 books in her lifetime with worldwide sales of over 1 billion copies and her books were translated into 36 different languages.

As well as romantic novels, she wrote historical biographies, 6 autobiographies, theatrical plays, books of advice on life, love, vitamins and cookery. She also found time to be a political speaker and television and radio personality.

She wrote her first book at the age of 21 and this was called *Jigsaw*. It became an immediate bestseller and sold 100,000 copies in hardback and was translated into 6 different languages. She wrote continuously throughout her life, writing bestsellers for an astonishing 76 years. Her books have always been immensely popular in the United States, where in 1976 her current books were at numbers 1 & 2 in the B. Dalton bestsellers list, a feat never achieved before or since by any author.

Barbara Cartland became a legend in her own lifetime and will be best remembered for her wonderful romantic novels, so loved by her millions of readers throughout the world.

Her books will always be treasured for their moral message, her pure and innocent heroines, her good looking and dashing heroes and above all her belief that the power of love is more important than anything else in everyone's life.

"Love has always been the guiding star of my life."

Barbara Cartland

CHAPTER ONE
1870

The Earl of Bracken walked into White's Club in St.James's Street.

"Good morning, my Lord," the porter greeted him.

"Good morning, Jackson," the Earl replied. "Is Captain Kenwood here yet?"

"No, my Lord, but there's a letter for you that has just arrived."

He produced a sky blue envelope and the Earl took it from him and put it in his pocket before walking into the coffee room.

There were two members of the Club whom the Earl knew well sitting in the bow window which had been made famous by Beau Brummel.

They were deep in conversation and he had no wish to join them, so he walked quickly to the other end of the room and sat down in a corner.

He ordered a bottle of champagne from the Steward and almost reluctantly opened the letter which had been waiting for him.

It was, as he knew, from Lady Grantham as there was a faint scent emanating from the paper which he recognised.

He considered it a mistake for Irene to write to him using anything so noticeable as her sky blue writing paper. She had made it specially her own and the Earl knew it was recognised by the porters in his Club as well as by most servants in houses in Mayfair.

As he expected the letter was a long effusion of love and was mingled with urgent requests for him to come to her as quickly as possible.

He read it through and tucked it away into his pocket.

It was increasingly obvious that Irene Grantham was becoming somewhat of a problem and one that he was finding increasingly difficult to solve.

After the Earl had travelled round the world at his father's suggestion, he had returned to England looking for amusement and it had not been hard to find.

As he was exceedingly handsome, well off and heir to the Dukedom of Brackenshaw, he was on the list of every Society hostess.

He was also on the list of ambitious mothers of daughters they hoped would make a good matrimonial catch.

The Earl had long ago been determined not to marry until he was very much older. Although he was the heir to this father's title, he had a brother who would take his place if he did not produce a son.

He made it very clear to his relatives that if he did marry it would be his own choice and he did not need their advice nor to be in any way pushed into matrimony.

What happened next was inevitable.

A large number of attractive and colourful married ladies had made London Society the talk of Europe, and the Earl had quickly found one amongst them who fascinated him.

When he had first seen Irene, he had recognised that

she was different from the women he had met on his travels.

They gravitated towards each other almost instinctively.

Very slim, with dark hair and flashing green eyes, Irene was sinuous and exotic. She fastened herself, as it were, around any man she fancied.

He found it impossible either to ignore her or to move away.

As soon as she met the Earl she knew at once that he was exactly what she had been looking for. She had been married when she was just eighteen to Lord Grantham.

He was old enough to be her father, but was anxious to produce a son and an heir.

He also found Irene irresistible.

He had been married to a woman who was a perpetual invalid and he had found her extremely boring only a few months after they were married.

When she died he told himself that if he married again it would be his choice and not that of his relatives.

He had fallen head over heels in love, as only an elderly man can, when he was first introduced to Irene.

Her father was a country Squire from a well known and respected family but with very little money.

He and his wife were overwhelmed and delighted when Lord Grantham started to woo their daughter, conveniently ignoring the difference in their ages.

Irene had been ambitious from the moment she was born. She had always desired more from life and she was determined to outshine her friends and her relations.

Lord Grantham had then proposed to her.

She realised that he could take her away from the parochial boredom of the country to the bright lights of Mayfair.

As soon as they were married Irene began to shine as a London hostess and she found that most of her husband's friends, although they were elderly, were members of the House of Lords.

Her parties which were lacking in the younger generation became noted for their intelligent conversation and there was always a variety of nationalities amongst her guests.

Irene was not well read nor particularly well educated. She was however clever enough to be able to draw a man out and to make him feel that everything he said to her was of vital interest.

It soon became an honour to be invited to dinner by the Granthams and invitations to Irene's parties were particularly sought after, especially amongst diplomats.

She was however insatiable where a man she fancied was concerned.

If Lord Grantham was ever suspicious that she had taken a lover, he did not appear to suffer from jealousy and nor did he interfere with his wife's pleasures.

Irene flirted with practically every man she met and they swarmed over her like bees around a honey-pot.

Lord Grantham actually took it all as rather a compliment to himself.

It was not surprising that the young Prince of Wales soon became one of Irene's guests, nor that practically every distinguished gentleman in London was seen sooner or later at his Lordship's table.

Irene had however never lost her heart as she controlled her emotions by not allowing them to control her.

That was until she met the Earl of Bracken at a dinner party given by the Duchess of Devonshire.

Favin Bracken had been invited soon after he returned

4

to London and he had accepted more out of curiosity than because he enjoyed large dinner parties.

Having been abroad for so long he wanted to compare the parties in London with those which he had attended in India, Egypt, St.Petersburg and New York.

He was thinking that such grandiose occasions on the whole were all much of a muchness when he was introduced to Irene.

She was certainly very beautiful.

He understood exactly what she was feeling when their eyes met and in fact it was happening to them both in the same instant.

There were plenty of acquaintances to tell him the next day and every day all they knew about Irene. The gossips, the majority of whom were jealous, were none too kind in what they related.

From the Earl's point of view it merely made her even more attractive as she was a challenge which had been difficult for him to resist.

What he had not expected was that Irene would fall wildly in love with him, which was not only overwhelming but, he felt, somewhat dangerous.

Lord Grantham was prepared to close his eyes to indiscretions, which could not be proved and gossip which was always exaggerated. He was however an intelligent man and exceedingly proud of his family and lineage.

It was of course the unwritten law of Society that there should be no scandal and that a married woman should never damage her husband's reputation by besmirching hers.

Where Favin Bracken was concerned, Irene pursued him relentlessly making it abundantly clear that she loved him as she had never loved a man in her life.

She wrote him smouldering letters which he burned

immediately as he was afraid that they might fall into the wrong hands, which could do both her and him an enormous amount of damage.

She pursued him wherever he was staying and she begged him to come to her husband's house.

At times the Earl thought it would not only be indiscreet but madness to agree.

"We have to be careful, Irene," he said not once but a dozen times.

"I love you, Favin," Irene simpered. "There has never been anyone like you. Oh, darling, why did we not meet before I married?"

There were many answers the Earl could have given her, one being that she had been married for six years. He would at that time have only just been coming down from Oxford and he would have possessed very little then to recommend him in Irene's ambitious eyes.

His father had been the Earl of Bracken and he was allowed very little money by the reigning Duke, so that Favin was in fact extremely hard-up.

He was well aware of Irene's extravagance.

The large parties she gave incessantly in London and in the country would have been far beyond his meagre purse as a young man.

Two years after her marriage Irene was beginning to climb the social tree and it was then that Favin's father became the Duke of Brackenshaw.

He, as the eldest son boasted the courtesy title of the Earl of Bracken. However money was still scarce.

After three years in the family Regiment, which was an expensive one, Favin resigned his Commission in the Army and on his father's instructions he set off to explore the world.

The first time he returned was largely to collect more money as he was always short. Afterwards it was to be with his father who was in ill-health.

It was only when Favin returned last year that he began to take charge of the Ducal estate as his father was no longer capable of doing anything.

Now that he had introduced modern farming methods on the estate, the situation had begun to improve.

And then he met Irene!

It was only with the greatest difficulty that he managed to prevent her from taking up all his time.

Having read Irene's letter, the Earl deliberately lit a match and burned it piece by piece in one of the ashtrays on the table in front of him.

He had disposed of the last corner of the blue writing-paper when the Steward brought him the champagne he had ordered. Having set it down on the table the Earl removed the ashtray.

"Shall I pour you out a glass, my Lord?" the Steward enquired. "Or will you wait for your guest?"

"Give me half a glass now, please."

He was sipping the champagne slowly when Captain Charles Kenwood came hurrying across the room.

"I am sorry I am late," he said as he sat down beside the Earl. "I have been at Tattersall's to look at some horses, but I regret to say that they all fetched more than I could afford."

"It's about horses that I would like to talk to you," the Earl began.

Charles Kenwood was a good-looking young man but not as outstandingly handsome as the Earl. They had been at Eton together and next at Oxford and they had actually joined the same Regiment at the same time.

Charles had stayed on after the Earl had resigned his Commission. He had in fact only left six months ago after his father had died.

Then he had gone to the country to look after his estate and his younger sister.

Charles's father had been General Sir Alexander Kenwood and had commanded the Household Cavalry.

He was not a rich man by any means but he owned an attractive house on a five hundred acre estate in Hertfordshire.

It was very different from the enormous mansion in Huntingdonshire which had been in the Earl's family since the time of Henry VIII.

All down the centuries the Brackens had always been distinguished members of the Establishment. They had improved and added to their home which became one of the most outstanding ancestral houses in England.

It was only now, the Earl thought with pride, that under his orders and guidance the estate was again profitable.

Over the centuries his family had been able to accumulate one of the finest collections of pictures and furniture in England.

As Charles Kenwood sat down beside him, the Earl asked him,

"Were you surprised to receive a letter from me?"

"I was delighted," Charles answered. "I heard you were back and working hard on your estate, besides of course enjoying yourself in the social world."

There was a faint note of mockery in his voice, which told the Earl that the gossip about him and Irene had reached as far as Hertfordshire.

The Earl poured out a glass of champagne for his friend and refilled his own.

8

"Now listen, Charles, I need your help. And I feel only you can help me."

Charles Kenwood raised his eyebrows but did not reply.

"One or two friends have told me," the Earl continued, "what excellent horses they have bought from you recently that you have broken in and trained yourself."

Charles nodded. "It is something, as you know, I have always enjoyed. When my father died I had to leave the Regiment and make enough money to keep my estate going and provide both for my sister and myself."

"Which I am sure you have done admirably," the Earl declared. "And as I am sure you are aware, I have been doing very much the same thing – *when I have been in the country.*"

He emphasised the last words.

Charles looked at him sharply.

"Are you in trouble, Favin?" he enquired.

There was a slight hesitation before the Earl replied,

"Shall I say I am standing on the edge of a precipice, and if I make one wrong step it might be disastrous."

Charles Kenwood sat back in his chair.

"What are you going to do about it?"

"That is what I am about to ask *you*."

Charles looked surprised. However with his usual tact he did not press the question.

He merely waited knowing his friend was choosing his words with care.

After a moment the Earl resumed,

"We are both keen on horses for our own enjoyment and are keenly aware that they also bring in the money we both need to develop our estates."

"That is true," Charles agreed. "It is why I visited Tattersall's this morning. Today I was a buyer and not a seller."

"But you have bought nothing?"

Charles shook his head.

"Quite frankly I thought the prices were too high and for that sort of money I would expect much better horseflesh."

"That is exactly what I wanted you to say! Because I have a suggestion which I think would be of great advantage to us both."

Charles looked interested.

"When I was travelling round the world," the Earl said, "I visited Syria. Of course you know, as I do, that the best horses of Arab blood come from that country."

Charles nodded before he added,

"And it is almost impossible today to buy a horse with Arab blood in it without paying an astronomical price."

"That is just what I find and why it is important for you and me to take advantage of the opportunity to bring back to England the finest Arab thoroughbreds in the world."

Charles stared at him.

"What are you talking about?" he asked. "I do not understand you."

"When I was in Syria recently, I spent some time in Damascus, where I met an extremely interesting man."

Charles was now listening intently.

"I was told that he owned some very fine Arab horses. In fact almost the finest, which is saying a great deal for that country."

"I know what you are talking about," Charles said. "I was always told that *Bint el Ahwaya* is the breed belonging to the children of Ishmael, from which all genuine Arab horses have descended."

"That is indeed true and what I was looking for. Not to buy, as I had very little money in those days, but to admire."

"I do not blame you, as it is what I would enjoy myself. As you know it is very difficult to find a really good Arab horse in England."

"I managed," the Earl continued, "to get to know a man in Syria called Sheik Abu Hamid."

He paused to ask without words if Charles had ever heard of him. His friend shook his head.

"He has built himself a large house not far from Damascus and he possesses the most marvellous Arab horses I have ever seen."

"You were very lucky," Charles murmured. "I would love to see them myself."

"They were fantastic and, I think because I was English and he liked me, he showed me every horse in his stable and there were a great number of them."

"I wish I had been with you," Charles remarked fervently.

"That is just what I want you to be."

Charles looked at him in astonishment.

"In Syria?"

"Exactly. Now listen while I explain. I asked the Sheik although at the time I had of course very little money on me, if he would sell me one of his horses. He shook his head and told me, 'I have no wish to sell any of my horses,' he said. 'I do not need the money and I like them with me.'

"Jokingly I asked how I could tempt him. The Sheik looked at me as if he knew my pockets were empty but at the same time thinking I might be useful to him. 'I will tell you,' he said at last, 'exactly what you can do for me'."

"What was that?"

"I wondered myself. 'You see that horse over there,' the Sheik said. He pointed and I saw one of the finest Arab stallions I could have ever imagined."

The Earl paused for a moment as if he was looking back into the past and then he said in a dreamy voice,

"He was a beautiful bay with black points, over fifteen hands high with large pointed ears. He had two white feet and a blaze down his nose."

"What price would you have had to pay for him?" Charles enquired.

"I knew it was something so astronomical that it was a stupid question, but all the same I asked."

"And how did the Sheik reply?"

"He took a little time and then he said, 'as perhaps you know, I am not entirely a Bedouin. My father was one, which is why I call myself a Sheik. But my mother was half Spanish with, I think, some Egyptian blood in her'."

"You must have wondered what this had to do with the stallion," Charles commented.

"I did but I was wise enough to keep silent and the Sheik continued, 'they respect me here, but I am well aware that I am unimportant in comparison to Sheik Abdul Medjvel el Mezrab. He is a Bedouin Chief of one of the largest tribes in Syria and is married to a very beautiful and famous Englishwoman.'"

The Earl paused as if he was looking back.

He knew that Charles would remember the extraordinary story of the Lady Jane Digby who had astounded the social world with her beauty.

She was married first to Lord Ellenborough, who was later to become Governor-General of India. After four years she had left him for an Austrian Prince – a separation which led to one of England's most scandalous divorce cases.

However the beautiful Jane was not content with her Prince for long. She in turn left him and moved to the Court of King Ludwig of Bavaria. There she married a Baron only to leave him for a Greek Count and later an Albanian brigand.

London Society talked of nothing but Jane and her lovers.

In her forties Jane took the last step which astounded social circles of several countries.

She fell wildly in love with a Bedouin Sheik and after marrying him she lived with him in the Syrian Desert.

She followed her husband into battle in his many tribal wars.

She was, the Earl was told, still beautiful and admired by almost every man who met her.

"When the Sheik spoke of her," the Earl resumed, "I told him that of course I knew the extraordinary history of the beautiful Jane Digby, but asked what it had to do with his horses.

"'A great deal, if you are really interested in them', the Sheik replied. I looked at him finding him hard to follow until he said, 'because I want to win the same admiration and respect that is paid to Sheik el Mezrab and the only way I can do so, is if I am visited by a Royal Princess and receive her as my guest.'

"As you can imagine I stared at him in astonishment. I could not believe what he was saying. 'A Royal Princess!' I exclaimed, 'but how could that help you?'

"'It would enhance my reputation,' the Sheik replied, 'and although the beautiful Lady Jane has married a number of different men, she is not a Princess of the Royal blood. That is what I require.'

"I could not think what to say to him. It flashed through my mind that if I could take him a Princess to stay in his house, then he would allow me to buy some of his priceless stallions, which in my opinion are worth a great deal more than any Royalty!"

Charles laughed.

"I doubt if they would agree with you but at the same time what do you intend to do?"

"I have not, until now," the Earl answered, "had the money to buy anything as expensive as an Arab mare or stallion. But now that because my father has become incapable, I have taken complete control of the estate and I find I am a great deal richer than I thought I was!"

"That is great news," Charles remarked.

"Money was being lost because the ground was not fully cultivated and some of our capital was not even invested as it should have been."

He paused for a moment before he said,

"This may surprise you, Charles, but I am now a rich man with the likelihood of being very much richer still."

"I congratulate you."

"I don't want your congratulations. What I want is your assistance in finding and taking a Royal Princess to the Sheik and bringing back at least half-a-dozen horses."

Charles gasped audibly but the Earl carried on,

"I will breed from them and astound the English owners because my horses will be so very much superior to theirs."

"It all sounds fantastic, but I cannot think where you are going to find a Royal Princess who will travel with you to Syria. But of course I should be only too thrilled to breed from the Arab horses and run them in all the Classic races."

"That is what I definitely intend to do and that is why, Charles, you have to find me a Princess."

"Me!" Charles exclaimed. "How on earth do you think I can do that?"

The Earl looked over his shoulder just to make sure that they were still alone in their corner of the room. A few more members had come into the Club while they were talking, but they were however all clustered round the bow-window.

"A Princess is a Princess," he said quietly, "but what we need to find is someone who will impersonate one so convincingly that the Sheik will not be suspicious."

"It is impossible," Charles moaned. "Someone is bound to spot it if we arrive with a Princess who is a phoney."

"Why should they?" the Earl objected. "You know as well as I do that Queen Victoria boasts dozens of her family on thrones all over Europe."

Charles had to admit this was true.

"A great number of those young women," the Earl said, "are cousins and distant relatives. No one had ever heard of them until they were paired off with some Balkan Prince who ruled over a small Principality he did not want the Russians to get their hands on."

Charles laughed, yet he could not deny it.

The Russians had been gradually infiltrating into the Balkans and by causing trouble in small countries and deliberately inciting revolts and uprisings, they had moved in on the pretence of restoring peace.

It had therefore become a regular resort for the Ruler of an endangered small country to apply to Queen Victoria for help.

If she sent him an English Princess, it meant that from

then on the country became under the protection of Great Britain.

The Russians, at this moment, had no desire for another war and it was thus quite true to say that where the Union Jack waved, the Russians kept well away.

Aloud Charles said,

"I do not know quite what you are suggesting. Do you want me to find a real Princess or an actress to impersonate one and be clever enough to make the Sheik believe in her?"

"The latter seems to be the only solution," the Earl responded. "Queen Victoria will certainly not lend one of her precious grandchildren to a mere Sheik."

He made an impressive gesture with his hands before he added,

"No one is going to believe that he has any Royal blood in his veins. In fact if the truth be told, his horses are better bred than he is!"

Charles chuckled.

"That I can believe. So what are you asking me to do is to find you a bogus Princess."

"She must be pretty, a lady, well-behaved and intelligent enough," the Earl replied, "to make the Sheik, if no one else, believe her to be Royal."

"It sounds impossible," Charles demurred.

"Nonsense! I can think of a dozen young women, who, if we took them to Damascus would look like English Royalty amongst a crowd of Bedouins."

"I would not like to bet on it, but I am prepared to believe you."

The Earl poured them each out another glass of champagne.

"Now be sensible, Charles, I mean this seriously and I need those horses badly. Can you imagine what a success we would have with first class Arab horses? I can promise you they are far superior to anything I have ever seen in this country."

"You are making my mouth water," Charles complained. "But I can still see it will be very difficult and most young women would think it an insult to be asked to deceive a Sheik."

"You can always point out to them what a success Jane Digby is being," the Earl replied. "And do not forget that her husband, Sheik Abdul Medjvel el Mezrab is in fact an Arab nobleman."

"Are there really such things," Charles asked rather scornfully.

"I can promise you, his blood is as blue as that of his wife. In fact amongst his own people it is even considered that his marriage is a *misalliance*."

Charles put his hand on his forehead.

"It is all too complicated for me, but I am still yearning for those horses. Oh, come on, Favin, think of a better way we can acquire them."

"I can assure you that there is no other way. Quite frankly I am prepared to buy half-a-dozen if not more, once the Sheik will allow us to do so."

"You really think that all we have to do is to produce a Royal Princess?"

"When the Arabs make up their minds about something, they are determined that in some incredible way their dream will come true."

He paused for a moment before he added,

"In this case *my* dream will come true too."

"I can see that you envisage Brackenshaw Hall in the future will be surrounded by Arab horses and you and I will be riding around like Kings," Charles teased.

17

"I shall feel like Apollo or one of the other Gods once I can get my hands on those horses. Now, come on, Charles, it cannot be so difficult for you to think of some girl who will help us."

"I should have thought Irene Grantham might be more helpful that I can be," Charles ventured.

As he spoke he realised that he had made a mistake.

His friend frowned.

"Whatever happens," he reacted in a low voice, "it is most important that Irene should not find out what we are planning."

"Why ever not?"

The Earl hesitated before he replied and Charles wondered if he would tell him the truth.

Then as if he thought it was the best way forward, he remarked,

"One of the reasons I am anxious to be away from England for a time is that I am walking on dangerous ground and I do not like it."

"I can understand that," Charles said quickly, "and of course I was only joking."

"Irene is no joke. In fact to be honest with you, Charles, as you are my oldest friend, she intends by hook or by crook to marry me."

"Marry you?" Charles exclaimed. "But she is already married!"

"Her husband drinks when he is tired and she has even suggested that he might fall from the battlements of his castle which, as you may know, is a very ancient one."

Charles stared at him.

"Fall!" he exclaimed after a moment. "Do you mean – "

"It is just a suggestion, but it is something which

makes me think it would be a good idea if I left England for some time."

Charles had indeed met Irene.

He had thought that the way she behaved with the Earl was likely to lead to trouble.

Now he said quickly,

"In that case the sooner we depart the better."

"I agree with you, but it would be quite useless going without our Princess."

There was silence.

Then the Earl pleaded,

"Oh, for God's sake, Charles, help me! I need help and it really seems as if the whole idea is a lifebelt thrown to me when I was drowning."

Charles drew in his breath.

He had always been extremely fond of Favin and he realised now that somehow he must help him. A friendship of so many years could not be ignored.

But for the moment his mind was blank.

Then as he was about to send up a prayer for help, he had an idea.

It seemed so preposterous that he did not say it aloud.

Then, because he knew him so well, the Earl became conscious of his thoughts.

"You have come up with something. I knew you would, Charles. You have never failed me yet and you have pulled me out of such a lot of trouble since we were first at school together."

Charles knew this to be true.

He had covered up for his friend at school when he had disobeyed the rules and he had warned him when he was unaware of danger from the prefects and the Masters.

In the Army there had been moments when Favin would have been in a great deal of trouble if Charles had not lied and saved him.

"I have an idea," he began as the Earl waited impatiently, "but I am not at all confident that it will work."

"What is it?"

"It is," Charles said reluctantly, "that I might persuade – my sister to play – the part of – the Princess."

CHAPTER TWO

Vanda Kenwood was riding through the Park. She was thinking as she did so that the grounds needed plenty of attention.

They were short-handed on the estate and it meant that the men did not find time to tidy up under the old oak trees.

Some were shedding branches and Vanda had to tread carefully or her horse might trip over one.

However she was always happy when she was riding in the Park. Not only because it was so old, but it had grown more beautiful year by year.

The house was very much the same. The old bricks had mellowed with the ages and although the roof was constantly in need of repair, the ancient building portrayed a beautiful symmetry.

The Kenwoods had lived in Hertfordshire for many generations.

Although they were not of great social importance, they were respected by their neighbours and their tenants and employees spoke of them with affection.

Vanda often thought that this was more important than anything else.

"They love you, Papa," she would say to her father when he was alive, "and when you are ill or worried the whole village is thinking of you and praying that you will soon be better."

Her father had smiled.

At the same time Vanda knew that this was the compliment he preferred to any other.

A handsome man, he had been very much in love with his wife when he married her.

It was not surprising, he often thought, that their daughter was so beautiful, although hers was not the sophisticated beauty which his son and the newspapers told him was so much admired in London.

The social beauties who attracted the attention of the Prince of Wales had become famous, much more so than had ever happened in the past.

In fact, as General Kenwood often said, it had been considered vulgar in his day for a lady's name to appear in the newspapers with the exception of when she was born and when she died.

Vanda however was not concerned with anything that was happening in London.

Her beloved father had died three years ago and her brother had left his Regiment and returned home to look after the estate.

Charles had made plans with her mother that when she was eighteen Vanda should come out as a *debutante* in London and would be presented at Court, as was expected of ladies who were well born.

Lady Kenwood however had died the previous winter.

It had been very cold and her sore throat had eventually turned to pleurisy. Vanda and her brother Charles were stricken by their loss.

The whole village of Little Medway mourned too and even the smallest child managed to collect a few flowers or berries to place on her grave.

As Vanda said to her brother at the time,

"Mama was a mother to them all in the same way as she was to us."

"It is just what you will have to be now," Charles replied.

Vanda did not contradict him.

She was friends with everyone in the village in the same way as her father and mother had been. She would call on them if they were ill or celebrating anything as exciting as a wedding or a new baby.

If they were in trouble they always came to the Manor to ask for advice from either the General or his wife.

Now Vanda was attempting to take her mother's place and as Charles had told her more than once, she was doing so very well.

As the Park came to an end, she was now facing the Manor which she thought looked so lovely in the evening sunshine, but it did need a great deal of attention.

The winow frames should be painted and there was brickwork near to the roof of the house which was in urgent need of restoration.

'I will talk to Charles about it,' Vanda told herself.

She rode up to the house and then turned towards the stables.

They employed three stable boys as well as old Andrew, who had been with the family for more years than anyone could remember. He was as fond of the horses as they were, and was always ready to look after new purchases.

"Andrew does three men's work," Vanda had often said to her mother who agreed with her.

At the same time Vanda recognised that if Charles

brought back another horse or perhaps two from the sales at Tattersall's, they would need to employ at least one more boy. That meant of course that they would have to economise in some other direction.

She tried to think what these economies could possibly be.

She knew even if it was extravagant, that Charles would buy new horses whenever he had the chance, but he had made a good profit from his horse-trading in the past year.

He had broken in some young horses and sold them for at least four times more than he had paid for them. Equally his horses cost in proportion rather more than anything else on the estate.

Yet as Vanda had said so often,

"They are worth every penny we spend on them, even more than we spend on ourselves."

Charles knew she was speaking sincerely as it was just what he felt too.

Their father had been an outstanding rider and both children had ridden from the moment they could walk.

Charles enjoyed watching his sister. He knew there was no one he had seen on the hunting-field to rival her.

The beauties of Mayfair trit-trotting in Rotten Row were undoubtedly impressive, yet they would, he thought, be useless at riding over rough ground as he and Vanda would enjoy every day.

There was always a great deal to be done on the estate, because they could not afford to employ as many men as they really required.

The crops had been good last year and when Charles had looked carefully at his bank balance to see if he could afford it, he had driven to London to buy a new horse.

"Make it two," Vanda pleaded.

She knew, although he made no promises, that he would not forget her wishes.

Vanda reached the old stables which had been built many centuries ago on the cobbled yard.

Andrew came out to meet her.

"What time be ye expectin' Master Charles?" he asked.

Because he had been with the family for so long Andrew still called him 'Master Charles' despite the fact that he had been promoted Captain before he left the Army and was now in his twenty-sixth year.

"He will be here for dinner," Vanda told Andrew, "and I do hope his journey has been successful."

"Oi got the stables ready for 'em," Andrew replied.

"I felt sure that you would have done," Vanda smiled.

She slipped off the saddle and patted her horse.

It was the one she loved more than any of the others, but he was growing old and she knew that if she was to continue to ride every day with Charles, she must sooner or later acquire another mount.

She patted Swallow again and said to him,

"Whatever Captain Charles brings back, there will never be anyone as wonderful as you, so you must not be jealous!"

"That be true," Andrew agreed. "Swallow's done ye well, Miss Vanda, but it's only fair as he be gettin' on he must take things more easy."

"And that applies to you as well," Vanda replied. "My brother has already said we must be looking for another boy to help you if there are to be any more horses in the stables."

"Oi be managing all right at the moment, Miss Vanda,"

but Oi'll not say nay to a helpin' 'and if there be any more 'orses."

"And you know as well as I do, Andrew, that he will want you to handle any new horses that need breaking in."

Andrew smiled at her as she walked away.

'We are so lucky,' she thought, 'to have these old servants who have been with Mama and Papa. They look after Charles and me as if we were small children.'

She reached the door of the house.

The old butler who had been at the Manor for nearly thirty years came into the hall.

"Have you had a nice ride, Miss Vanda?" he asked.

"A lovely one, Johnson, and I am hoping Captain Charles will be back soon."

"I've just said to the Missus," Johnson replied, 'Master Charles will be wanting the special soup you makes for him tonight. That be something he can't get in London as us all knows'."

"You are quite right, Johnson, and I too enjoy her wonderful soup."

As she walked up the stairs Vanda understood that her words would be relayed back to the kitchen.

If there were to be any new horses and they were indeed expensive, she must forget that the carpet was almost threadbare. She had already told Charles several times that they needed a new one.

She walked into her bedroom.

It was a very attractive room overlooking the garden and the sun was shining through the diamond-paned windows.

Vanda noticed that the old maid who looked after her had arranged the flowers she had picked that morning in a blue vase on her dressing table

Next to her horses, Vanda loved flowers more than anything else. She spent as much time as she could spare helping in the garden.

She often complained that it was where Charles economised because there was no profit to be made from the garden.

"It is the money that counts," he would comment.

Vanda knew that he was only teasing but she always retorted,

"Think of the happiness the garden gives us and you cannot put that into pounds, shillings, and pence!"

The last time she said it Charles had laughed and put his arms around her.

"You shall have your flowers," he promised, "but I cannot afford to build you a new greenhouse this year."

"The old one is so congested I can hardly move inside it," Vanda protested. "If you say, 'next year,' to me again, I shall try to think up some way that *I* can make money."

Charles had replied scornfully,

"How do you suggest you can do that? Giving riding lessons to young children or asking men like myself what they will pay for dancing lessons?"

Vanda had laughed.

"That is not a bad idea, except that you dance so well already, I do not think I could teach you very much. But of course I might dance on the stage."

She twirled round as she spoke.

She allowed her dress to flare out to reveal her very pretty ankles.

Watching her, he was struck again that her beauty was being wasted.

She should be the toast of the young bloods that assembled every night at White's Club to discuss the latest beauty in London who had appeared in the Social world.

There was at the moment a great deal of talk about the '*Pretty Horsebreakers*,' as they were called and it flashed into Charles's mind that quite a number of country girls like his sister were amongst them.

The *Pretty Horsebreakers* were in fact an endless topic of conversation. They were new and had not appeared on the social scene until very recently.

It was obvious that the young Ladies of fashion had to ride horses which were well broken in.

This was essential for the girls who had not had the advantage, as Vanda had, of having a father who was an outstanding rider.

When they came to London for the Season and to be presented to Her Majesty Queen Victoria, they were reluctant to ride in Rotten Row.

They knew that they would compare poorly with experienced riders who were mostly older married women who had been outstanding in the hunting fields for many years.

The Livery stables therefore found there was a great demand for quiet and well-trained horses, so that the young *debutantes* would have no difficulty in managing them.

An eager search began around the country for riders who could control a horse however difficult with surprisingly successful results.

Vicars' daughters had learned to ride any mount however badly trained and farmers' daughters had broken in horses for their father and brothers when they were too busy to do so themselves.

They were all delighted to be paid by the Livery stables to ride horses which were in demand from the *Beau Monde* and soon, of course, it became the fashion to be 'a *Pretty Horsebreaker*.'

That was not to say that every horse which was paraded in Rotten Row by an extremely attractive young woman was for sale *with* the rider.

A few were of course.

But the '*Pretty Horsebreakers*' were very clever keeping themselves aloof from what they considered to be low class courtesans.

If a wealthy gentleman was determined to claim both the horse and the rider, he would expect to pay a very considerable sum for the pair.

Charles had been interested first in the horses and then like his contemporaries in some of the riders.

He looked again and again at his sister and the way she rode.

He knew she would be outstanding if she was fashionably dressed amongst all the *Pretty Horsebreakers*.

It was understood that on Sundays they congregated at the Achilles statue at Hyde Park Corner and there were always a great number of gentlemen to ride with them.

Charles had however learned his lesson very quickly.

The horses he observed around the Achilles statue were certainly beyond his purse and there was no necessity for him to speculate on the likely price of the rider.

He did not talk about the *Pretty Horsebreakers* to Vanda as he knew she was too innocent to understand and would be curious only about the horses.

He had however discussed them with a number of his acquaintances, especially his good friend Favin, the Earl of Bracken.

"I will certainly take a look at them when I have time," the Earl had commented. "But at the moment I am concerned only with Arbas, the stallion I *must* buy."

Charles now recalled this conversation as he sipped his champagne in White's.

He remembered of old what Favin was like when he wanted something. He found it impossible to concentrate on anything else until what he desired was safely in his hands.

Both of the men were aware that there had been an importation of Eastern blood into the bloodstock of England over a long period of time.

Charles was not at all surprised that, now the Earl could afford it, he required only the best.

At the same time he had already found that anything concerned with Arab breeding was terrifyingly expensive.

"As it so happens," he said to the Earl, "I was reading just the other day that in 1735 the price of what was called a 'Right-Arabian' was estimated at anything up to three thousand pounds."

The Earl did not reply and Charles had continued,

"The Sultan of Nassri once paid six thousand pounds each for mares and forty thousand pounds for one celebrated stallion!"

The Earl laughed.

"You know as well as I do that I could not pay that sort of money. That is why we must buy the bloodstock from a source which so far has not been tapped."

"Do you think your Sheik knows their real market worth?" Charles asked.

"If he does, I would not be surprised, and it would not particularly concern him. He has set his heart on welcoming a Royal Princess as his guest and that is what we must provide."

He sighed before he added,

"Surely it is easier than doling it out in large amounts of pounds, shillings and pence?"

This discussion was taking place after Charles had mentioned his sister as a possible candidate and as if he knew it was a delicate subject, the Earl had not immediately pursued it.

He had merely impressed on his friend over and over again what was required that somehow they needed to find a young woman who could act the part.

And then they would leave for Syria.

"We can travel in my yacht or rather my father's yacht which is now mine," the Earl suggested. "That will be much more comfortable than going by steamship or overland."

Charles appreciated this point as he had travelled occasionally in troopships which were always overcrowded and extremely uncomfortable.

Finally Charles realised that Vanda would be waiting for him and she would be worried that if he did not appear that something might be wrong.

He told the Earl that he must return to the country.

"I am staying in the family house in Park Lane," the Earl declared, "and I shall expect you both the day after tomorrow."

"Now wait a minute, I have not yet spoken to my sister. She may be horrified at the idea! Also be sensible, Favin, and realise she will need clothes."

He paused for a moment.

"Your Sheik is not going to be impressed if the so-called Princess arrives in rags and tatters or at best something very countrified. I really do think, Favin, that we ought to engage an actress."

"Do you know one who is clever enough to behave like a Princess, talk like one and look line one," the Earl demanded. "If you do, I will agree, but you know as well as I do that most of them have no idea of how to behave like a lady let alone Royalty."

Charles had to admit this was true.

"I have said I will talk to Vanda and if she agrees we will come straight to London tomorrow. As she has very good taste I am sure we will find the sort of clothes a Princess would wear. At the same time quite frankly I cannot afford to pay for them."

"I will pay," the Earl offered. "Whatever it costs I assure you that it will be less than what the Sultan gave for his celebrated stallion."

Both men laughed.

"I should hope so." Charles said. "And I do not think for a moment that Wellington paid anything abnormal for his chestnut Arab called Copenhagen."

"I remember hearing," the Earl said, "that no one could drive a harder bargain than the Iron Duke."

"With the doubtless exception," Charles remarked, "of Benjamin Disraeli, who you remember hunted for years on an Arab mare and boasted that he was always the best rider in the field when he did so."

"I remember that too," the Earl replied. "I have always wished I had been present when he jumped his Arab over a dinner table."

"If that is the sort of stunt you are going to do in the future," Charles said, "I must make it very clear it will not be over *my* dinner table."

The Earl made a gesture with his hands.

"What we have to buy first," he emphasised, "are the Arab mares and at least one stallion for each of us."

"I would completely agree with that idea."

"Then get on with it," the Earl ordered. "We are talking too much and doing too little. The sooner we are on our way to Syria the better."

Charles found it impossible not to be aroused by his friend's enthusiasm. Equally he was worrying on his way home, as he was driving the very fast team which he had brought to London.

He loved his sister.

He had always recognised that she was his responsibility and he must do everything he could to take the place of both their father and mother.

Because Vanda was in mourning, it had been impossible for her to come to London this Season, but Charles was determined she should attend a number of Hunt balls in the autumn.

She would be presented at Court next year, even if she was a little old for a *debutante*.

He was very conscious that if he had Arab progeny to sell, he could do so much more for Vanda than he could at the moment.

However he realised that both his father and mother would be shocked at the mere idea of her pretending to be a Royal Princess, even though it was only to hoodwink an unimportant Arab of whom no one had ever heard.

It was nearly time for dinner when Charles turned in at the gates of the Manor.

He knew that if no one else was annoyed with him for being late, Mrs. Johnson would be. She became agitated if the special dishes she had cooked for him were spoilt.

He drew up his team outside the front door.

One of the stable boys came hurrying from the stables as Vanda came running down the steps towards him.

"You are back!" she cried excitedly. "You are so late that I was afraid something had happened to you."

"I am quite safe and you must forgive me for being later than I intended."

As Charles put down the reins and stepped down, Vanda kissed him and as they walked towards the front door, she slipped her hand into his.

"Have you any good news to tell me?" she enquired.

"I have most unusual news, something you did not expect," Charles replied. "As it is going to take a little time to explain, give me a chance to wash my hands first."

"You can wash but you had better not change your clothes," Vanda told him. "Mrs. Johnson is fussing in case your special dishes are spoiled."

Charles laughed.

"I was thinking just that as I came down the drive."

"Then hurry, you know how hard she tries to please you."

Her brother ran up the stairs three at a time.

Vanda walked into the small but very pretty drawing room and she was wondering what he had to tell her.

She was hoping almost against hope that he had been able to buy the horses he fancied, but she was sure it was just a question of price.

If they were very expensive, how could they economise to find the extra money?

'Charles is so clever with horses,' she thought. 'If they are a little rough they will become quite different when he has trained them. There are always people wanting his horses because they are better trained than anyone else's.'

She was wondering if there would be a new horse for her to ride.

Then she heard him descending the stairs.

She met him in the hall and they walked into the dining room together.

"Exactly two minutes past eight!" Charles exclaimed. "You must admit that is a good effort. Short of flying I could not have come back any quicker."

"You have done splendidly," Vanda said, "and putting Mrs. Johnson's mind at rest is more important than anything else."

They both chuckled.

Then as Johnson brought in the soup, Vanda enquired,

"Did you see any old friends in London?"

"I saw someone I had not seen for some time."

"Who was that?"

"Favin Shaw who is now the Earl of Bracken."

"I remember him, of course I remember him, you were at Oxford together and I remember you both taking me out to luncheon once when Papa and I visited you."

"I do remember the occasion, but Favin is now the Earl of Bracken and his father, the Duke, is extremely ill."

"Then I suppose he will inherit the title?"

Charles nodded because his mouth was full of Mrs. Johnson's excellent pie.

Vanda waited until they had finished the next course and Johnson had left the room, before quizzing him,

"Was the Earl of any use to you? Did he say he wanted to buy some horses?"

Charles was being rather slow in telling her what had happened and that there was something unexpected about his visit.

"Favin, as I expect you know," Charles began, "because we have talked about him before, has been travelling round the world. Now he has returned home and has taken over the management of the whole estate from his father and he naturally wants to improve his bloodstock."

Vanda clasped her hands together.

"That is what I wanted to hear. Oh, Charles, that is wonderful and of course you bought the new horses at

Tattersall's which you were talking about."

"The horses were not good enough but actually Favin has a better idea."

"What is that?"

"That we should travel to Syria and buy what he tells me are exceptionally fine Arab horses directly from their owner."

Vanda gave a gasp of surprise.

"Go to Syria!" she cried. "Why did we not think of this idea before?"

"Because it would be too expensive and because we would not know, as Favin does, where the best horses are to be found."

"Of course it is a wonderful idea," Vanda enthused. "But can we afford it at present?"

Charles paused for a moment.

As he did so Johnson entered the room with the next course and he did not speak until they had helped themselves.

When once again they were alone, Vanda urged him,

"Go on, Charles. I know you did not want to talk about going away in front of Johnson. But I am so curious that I am finding it difficult to breathe until I hear the end of your story."

"The end of the story becomes a little difficult because it concerns *you*."

Vanda opened her blue eyes very wide.

"Concerns me, but how can it?"

"Because Favin wants you to come with us, but *in disguise*."

Vanda stared at him.

"Is this a joke?" she asked.

"No, of course not, it is very serious. But I am afraid you will find it difficult to do what Favin wants, in which case we will just have to refuse."

"What does he want?" Vanda quizzed him expectantly. "And why is it so difficult?"

Charles looked over his shoulder before he spoke.

The door of the dining room was closed and anyway Johnson was slightly deaf.

"He wants you to come with us to provide what the Sheik who owns the horses requires and insists on. You are to pretend to be a Royal Princess!"

Vanda gulped.

"You don't really mean it?"

"Of course I mean it," Charles replied almost sharply. "I have been talking about the idea for hours. But there is no other way that Favin and I can acquire the horses we both need and which he assures me are absolutely beyond compare with any Arabs he has seen anywhere else."

There was a poignant silence before Vanda commented breathlessly,

"Suppose I make a mistake – or say the wrong thing and the Sheik realises – that I am an impostor."

"There is no reason why he should uncover you." Charles replied. "And there is no reason for us to see anyone else but him. So you need not be afraid of being criticised or cross-examined."

Vanda sat silently as Charles continued,

"I do not want to press you because it is something I could not ask of anyone else I know, nor would it be safe to do so. But Bracken is desperate to purchase these magnificent horses and naturally it is what I want for our estate too."

"Why will their owner sell them only if you take him

a Royal Princess?" Vanda wanted to know.

"It's a long story, but apparently he is jealous because Jane Digby, of whom you may have heard, has married a Sheik who is a nobleman of great prestige, and is now of even greater importance because he has married an Englishwoman who is so beautiful."

"The Sheik does not want to marry me?" Vanda asked nervously.

"Of course not. He is old and not interested in women in *that* way. What he wants is to raise his standing in his own neighbourhood. He can think of nothing which will do that better than if a British Royal Princess visits him to inspect his horses. It is as easy as that."

"If you and the Earl help me," Vanda said thoughtfully, "I cannot see why I should be exposed or, worse still, disappoint the Sheik."

Her brother stared at her.

"Do you mean it? Do you *really* mean it?" he asked.

"Of course I mean it. You want the horses and I want above everything to visit Syria or anywhere where there are the Arab horses we have always talked about and admired ever since I can remember."

Charles gave a deep sigh.

"I was afraid you would reject the whole scheme as insane the moment I broached it."

Vanda laughed.

"I love being here at the Manor and am very happy. But at the same time you must realise that you have seen a great deal more of the world than I have, and of course your friend the Earl has travelled to all sorts of marvellous places.

"I have always dreamt about visiting Greece, seeing the Pyramids of Egypt and of climbing the Himalayas, but up to now it has only been a dream and I have to imagine it all from the books I read."

She took a deep breath.

"To see Syria would be to make my dreams come true!"

"Then it is settled," Charles stated with a tone of relief. "I thought you would never consider it for a moment, but I know when I take you to London tomorrow how grateful Favin will be."

Vanda stared at him.

"To London tomorrow?" she repeated.

"The sooner we start off on our voyage, the better. I don't mind telling you quite frankly I am half afraid, if we do not agree at once, that as Favin is so determined to return to Syria that he will engage some actress to go with him."

"We cannot allow him to do that. It will be the most exciting and the most thrilling thing I have ever done! Even if we cannot afford to buy many of the Arab horses, at least I shall have seen them and stepped into their world, which will be something to remember."

"We will buy a few if it costs every penny I possess," Charles vowed determinedly. "But I do know where Favin is concerned that we must act quickly. What time can you be ready to leave?"

"In ten minutes," Vanda teased him.

When she saw the expression on her brother's face she promised,

"To be serious, I will be ready at ten o'clock tomorrow morning and that will give us time to do some shopping before we leave the next day, if that is what the Earl is planning."

"You do realise you will need grand clothes."

"Of course I realise it. There are a few of Mama's dresses which I might be able to use, but they are slightly out of date, and as a Royal personage I cannot travel in rags and tatters."

"That is exactly what I said to Favin," Charles agreed. "He recognises that you will require some really smart clothes. As he has been in London for some time recently, he will know where we can shop. And doubtless, more than we do, what you will need."

"I have looked in the magazines at what Princess Alexandra and the other ladies wear," Vanda said, "and I am very conscious that my clothes are out of date. I shall need to buy some really lovely dresses, but you know as well as I do that they will be expensive."

"I will work out," Charles said, "exactly what we can spend, and I know that Favin will help me, because it is in his interest even more than in ours that we please the Sheik."

Vanda parted her lips to say it would be most improper to accept money from a gentleman if it was just a question of buying her clothes.

But she told herself that it would be silly to think like that.

It was a business proposition!

If the Earl was to purchase the Arab horses he coveted, he would have to produce a Royal Princess appropriately dressed for their owner.

It all seemed too extraordinary.

Yet from what she had read of the East and it was a great deal, many extraordinary things happened there which would never be tolerated or even considered in England.

'I must not make any difficulties,' she told herself. 'I must just accept events as they unfold and hope there will be no recriminations afterwards.'

It sounded rather alarming but on the other hand her heart was singing.

No one knew how much she longed to travel abroad and to experience a little of the world outside the small part of Hertfordshire where they lived.

It would be an adventure, a thrill and, as she had said to Charles, a dream come true.

She would be very stupid if she made any difficulties or if she behaved like a strictly brought up Society girl!

She had been told so often that was what she was expected to become, but she always thought of herself as someone very different.

As an essential part of the countryside, the trees and the crops, the streams running through the meadows and the flowers which filled the garden at the back of Manor.

This was Vanda's world.

But she was in a way confined by the smallness of it.

The images of her ancestors were as real to her as the people who were moving about the house at the moment.

Because she was so excited, her eyes were shining.

As they walked from the dining room back into the drawing room, she looked even prettier than she usually did.

In fact Charles became suddenly aware of his sister as a woman.

"You must understand, Vanda, that no ordinary Society lady should behave in this fashion and I think Mama would be very shocked at your doing anything so unconventional."

"It may be unconventional," Vanda replied, "but for me it is going to be something so exciting and so wonderful that I am just afraid everything will be cancelled at the last moment."

"I don't think that is likely, as Favin is desperate to get away as quickly as he can."

"Then we must not disappoint him," Vanda proposed. "I think in fact I can be ready by nine o'clock. I have very little which will be of much use to bring with me and you had better ask your friend to lend us some of the Brackenshaw jewellery for me to wear."

She paused for a few seconds,

"Mama's is very pretty but I do not think it is impressive enough if I have to impress a Sheik."

"That is very clever of you," Charles remarked. "I never thought of jewellery."

"Let us go to bed and think of everything we need to take with us from England," Vanda suggested. "If I am to act out this part successfully, we must arrange everything so cleverly that no one can ever be suspicious! That I think should include those who travel with us."

"We are travelling on Favin's yacht and that will make it very much easier than if we had to employ couriers and special carriages, which I have always understood are attached to trains when Royalty is travelling."

"It is certainly true if it includes the Queen."

"But you will just be a Princess and I am sure Favin will think of some way in which you can be supported."

"Of course you and the Earl will be on duty at all times. But what about Ladies-in-Waiting?"

"I am sure Favin will have considered them," Charles said optimistically. "But I will remind him just as soon as we reach his house in London, where we will be staying."

"If I am staying with him as your sister, you must not breathe a word to anyone, especially the servants that I am to be disguised later as a Princess."

"There I agree with you. It would be disastrous if anyone had the slightest idea what you are doing. Especially as Favin is the son of a Duke and all the social world likes to talk about Dukes."

"Well let them talk about him," Vanda said, "but not about me."

She walked across the room and back again before she cried enthusiastically,

"I can hardly believe it is true what you have said. But if it is, I know this is going to be a great adventure. Something I have so longed for and never thought would happen to me. Oh, Charles, it is all so exciting!"

She clung to his arm as she spoke.

Her brother thought she looked so pretty, but he was beginning to worry that such a journey might be dangerous for her and it was really something he should now allow.

But he realised that Vanda was so thrilled by the idea that he could not now tell her it was all a mistake.

Perhaps he should really ask the Earl to find someone else to act the part of the Princess.

Then he asked himself if he was not being too over-anxious. After all he and Favin were both there to keep a watch over Vanda so that no harm would come to her.

It was undoubtedly an opportunity for her to see the world which might never happen for her again.

Impulsively he put his arm round her.

"I will look after you, Vanda, and now as we have to leave early and have so much to do, I suggest you go to bed and try to sleep. I do not want you exhausted before we even start."

"I will definitely not be, and thank you, thank you, dearest Charles, for the most wonderful opportunity that has ever happened to me. You are the kindest and best brother in the whole wide world."

She kissed his cheek and ran towards the door.

"I will pack everything which might be useful," she said. "But I am afraid there is not much and you may have to spend a fortune to gain a fortune."

"I will manage somehow," Charles replied.

But already she was running down the passage towards the stairs.

CHAPTER THREE

The Earl had given a sigh of relief when Charles set off for the country. He had been concerned in case his friend would let him down at the last moment.

He felt sure that Charles's sister would enjoy the journey to Syria if nothing else. He therefore gave his valet instructions as to what to pack.

He sent a messenger to the Captain of his yacht to say that they would be leaving on Thursday morning.

He knew that the crew of the *Sea Serpent* would treat his orders as good news, as they had complained when his father was ill that they had nothing to do.

It was lucky, the Earl thought, that he had just arranged for the yacht to be overhauled and a great many new gadgets had been installed which had been introduced since his father had last put to sea.

There was only one matter left which compelled his attention and that was Irene.

He felt depressed at the very idea of telling her he was going away and he wondered how he could deceive her into thinking it was for only a short while, perhaps just a week.

He had however already planned to meet some of his friends at White's that evening, so he therefore postponed seeing Irene until the following day.

He realised that she expected him to visit her that very

evening as she had said in her letter that Lord Grantham had left for Windsor Castle.

'*We shall be alone, my darling,*' she wrote, '*and that as you know is all I could ever desire and is the most wonderful thing that could happen to me. Edward will not be back until Friday because there is to be a dinner party for some European dignitary. That means we can be together for three whole nights which is my idea of Heaven.*'

She carried on to write a great many more indiscreet words which made the Earl feel uncomfortable.

He had always thought it was for him to compose words of love and affection and certainly not the woman he was wooing.

He was acutely conscious that by this time Irene was indeed wooing him and everything that could be said about love she had already written in her letters.

He therefore decided that he would not tell her he was sailing away until the very last moment and that meant tomorrow evening and not tonight.

He enjoyed himself with his friends at White's Club and even won a little money on the gambling tables.

When he finally climbed into bed he felt he needed his sleep and all his wits about him.

If Charles returned from the country to say that his sister would not agree to the plan he had suggested, then he would have to think of someone else.

At the moment his mind was blank.

He had arranged an appointment with his Solicitors for the next morning and when he returned home for luncheon, he saw with a leap of his heart that Charles's travelling carriage was standing outside the door.

It was with difficulty that the Earl managed to ask in an ordinary calm manner of his butler,

"I think Captain Kenwood is here."

"Yes, my Lord, the Captain and his sister are in the library."

The Earl wondered why they were there as he hurried down the passage to the library which was at the far end of the house.

Both Charles and Vanda were resting open books on their knees as he entered the room.

"Oh, here you are, Favin," Charles greeted him. "We wondered when we arrived what had happened to you."

"I was seeing my Solicitors," the Earl answered, "but I am delighted you have returned and have brought your sister with you."

Vanda put down the book she was holding, rose to her feet and held out her hand.

"Charles has told me that you will take me to Syria," she enthused, "and it is the most exciting thing that has ever happened to me."

She paused and then asked the Earl,

"Are you sure he is not pulling my leg?"

"I can assure you that it is a very genuine invitation and if you accept the situation I am offering you, I will be more grateful than I can say."

Vanda gave a little laugh.

"I am only terrified that I shall fail you and you will be ashamed of me."

"I promise you that I will not be and I think it is very sporting and brave of you to undertake what your brother and I think is a very important mission."

"A mission to find the most fantastic Arab horses I will ever see?"

"That is indeed true," the Earl said. "When you see them you will realise they are far superior to any horse you have ever set your eyes upon."

"I can hardly believe that you will really take me with you," Vanda breathed.

"We have so much to do immediately we have finished luncheon," Charles said before the Earl could answer. "I am hoping you can give us the name of the best shop where we can purchase all we require."

"I have already written it down for you and I am sure that Madame Yvonne, who is French, will provide exactly what you need."

He was talking to Charles and at the same time he was looking at Vanda with astonishment.

He expected that she would be pretty from his memories of her as a child, but he had certainly not anticipated she would be so lovely!

Far lovelier than any woman he had seen for a long time.

She was, he thought, beautiful in a very different way from the beauties who were so admired and praised in the London social circles. He thought it was because she was small and slim and in a way more like a child than a woman.

Vanda had pulled off her hat when she and Charles were in the library as living in the country she seldom wore one.

The sun coming through the library windows turned her hair to gold and seemed to accentuate the perfection of her features which were almost classical.

Equally the fairy-like mystery of her blue eyes intrigued the Earl.

He thought himself somewhat of a connoisseur in women, but he had never seen eyes which seemed so mysterious and yet showed the clarity and purity of someone very young and innocent.

'She is certainly unique,' he thought to himself.

He noticed that Vanda's clothes looked as if they came from the country and obviously did not do justice to her figure.

The butler announced that luncheon was served.

In front of the butler and two footmen they discussed any subject except the one that really filled their minds and which was now more important than anything else.

Vanda talked of the improvements which Charles had made on their estate since he had left the Army.

The Earl told them all he had achieved since he had taken over the management of his ancestral lands and about the houses he owned in different parts of England.

"I have not touched the house we have in Newmarket yet," he said to Charles, "but I am hoping it is a place we shall need in the near future."

"I am sure we will," Charles replied, "but I am still keeping my fingers crossed."

"And I am doing the same," the Earl agreed.

Vanda thought that listening to their conversation was extremely interesting.

When they left the dining room she said,

"Now Charles and I must busy ourselves. Otherwise I am frightened you may leave without us."

"I would certainly not do so, but I should like to be away at the very latest tomorrow afternoon."

He was thinking as he spoke that their departure would prevent him having to be with Irene.

Charles gave a cry of horror,

"Come on, Vanda. We cannot stop here talking. Collect your hat and, Favin, please tell one of the footmen to call us a Hackney carriage."

While Vanda was putting on her hat, the Earl handed Charles an envelope.

"I thought it best," he whispered, "for you to pay in cash so that there would be no need for the shop to know who you are or to be curious about Vanda. A great number of fashionable ladies patronise Madame Yvonne. So she is inevitably one of the greatest gossips of Mayfair."

"We will be most discreet," Charles promised. "I can only hope that you will not be disappointed."

He tucked the envelope containing the money into his coat pocket.

A few minutes later they were driving away from Brackenshaw House.

When the Earl was on his own, he found that there were two letters in sky blue writing paper waiting for him. There was no need for him to question who they were from or what they may contain.

He merely sent a footman with a brief note to Irene telling her that he had returned to London, but he had guests staying with him and he therefore unfortunately could not go to see her this afternoon, but would call tomorrow morning about noon.

It was a brief formal note which if read by anyone but her would not cause any comment, but he was mistaken if he thought that Irene would accept such a plan.

An hour later as he was answering a number of letters with his secretary which had to be finished before he left England, when a note arrived from Irene which required an immediate answer.

She told him that even if he had all the Archangels in Heaven staying with him, she still intended to see him this evening.

'Come to me as soon as your guests have gone to bed,' she wrote. 'I shall be waiting for you. If you do not come to me, I will come to you. I am sure the night footman will let me in."

There was nothing the Earl could do but reply that he would pay her a visit as soon as dinner was completed. He did not dare make the assignation any later because undoubtedly the servants would talk.

He only hoped that Lord Grantham would not be told he had called at his house in his absence.

*

Vanda and Charles arrived at Madame Yvonne's emporium in Bond Street to find that it was even more luxurious and enticing than they expected.

Vanda had never seen such superb clothes and even Charles was forced to admit that they were smarter than anything he had seen on the famous beauties at London parties.

Because Vanda was so slim she fitted into a number of the model dresses, which came from Paris and were not usually sold to customers.

"We must not be too extravagant," Vanda murmured to Charles as Madame Yvonne was finding the clothes they had asked for.

"They are all a present from Favin," Charles told her. "You know I could not afford even one of them."

"He must be very rich," Vanda ventured. "At the same time we do not want to be too indebted to him."

"He thinks he is indebted to you, so you must look your very best and that cannot be achieved cheaply."

Vanda was delighted when Madame Yvonne showed her three new models which she said had just arrived from Paris.

They made her look, Charles thought, even more beautiful than she was already.

Finally they decided on four evening gowns and five different day dresses.

"Surely we shall not be staying as long as all that," Vanda muttered to her brother.

"I do hope not, but we must be prepared and after all a Royal Princess is a Royal Princess!"

Vanda giggled as she could not help it.

Charles insisted on buying a wrap for her to wear in the evening and a very smart coat in case it was cold when they were at sea.

Lastly, but most important were two riding skirts, which were very smart and French, more suitable, Charles considered, for the *Pretty Horsebreakers*.

However he felt that they would impress the Bedouins, so said nothing.

After the dresses they moved to the hat department.

Vanda looked so pretty in every hat she put on that finally Charles insisted on buying eight.

"They may not notice if you do not change your dress," he said, "but a hat is bound to attract attention."

By this time Vanda, who had never possessed more than one dress at a time and that was made by the village seamstress, was too bewildered to argue.

She convinced herself that the reflection she saw in the mirror could not really be herself.

Finally everything they had bought was packed up in neat parcels.

When Charles paid for it in cash, Vanda looked the other way as she did not want to be embarrassed by thinking how grateful she must now be to the Earl. Worse still how humiliated she would be if she was exposed.

It was getting on for six o'clock when they drove back to Park Lane.

Charles threw himself back in the Hackney carriage saying,

"If you are not exhausted, I am! I am so sorry for women that they have to endure all that dressing up."

"If you were a woman you would find it very stimulating," Vanda countered. "I still cannot decide if I am on my head or my heels or flying in the sky on a cloud!"

"You are going to have to work hard for everything you now possess," Charles warned her. "Do not forget for a moment that you are extremely important and you do not permit any impertinence from underlings like me!"

"It is going to be difficult, but I am sure I shall enjoy it."

It was not until later when they were waiting to go into dinner that Charles asked,

"Have you done anything about Ladies-in-Waiting or a chaperone? I forgot to ask you earlier. We cannot arrive in Syria just as we are."

"I have thought of everything," the Earl replied in a somewhat lofty tone. "The Captain of my yacht has a very pleasant wife whom he has wanted to take on voyages with him and the same applies to the Senior Steward. I have therefore told them to bring their wives with them tomorrow and that they are to act as Ladies-in-Waiting to Her Royal Highness who will be joining us."

"That is very bright of you," Charles admitted. "Have you told the Captain and the rest of the crew that Vanda is Royalty?"

"Of course I have. You know how servants talk especially when they are at sea. The Captain believes that Princess Vanda of Thessaly is coming aboard with us."

"Why Thessaly?" Charles enquired.

"Because I have told the Captain and also sent a

messenger ahead of us to Syria, that I am bringing with me Princess Vanda, the daughter of the late Prince Nikos of Thessaly. Her mother, Princess Louise, is English and a cousin of Her Majesty Queen Victoria and enjoys the privilege of a Grace and Favour house at Hampton Court."

Charles put his hand to his forehead.

"Really Favin, you should either be a best-selling author or a diplomat!"

"It took me a little time to work it all out but, as you know, Grace and Favour houses are mostly allocated to impoverished Royalty and diplomats. I have always thought they are treated very much as poor relations by Her Majesty."

"Of course it is doubtful if anyone knows who they are or where they come from," Charles added as if he was speaking to himself.

"That is indeed true, but you must make it clear to your sister that from the moment we leave this house tomorrow morning she is no longer herself."

When Vanda joined them the Earl repeated what he had already told Charles.

"I am so glad you left me with my own name," Vanda said. "It would be awful if you spoke to me and I thought you were talking to someone else."

"I have tried to make it as easy for you as I can and anyway I think Vanda is such a pretty name that it is indeed suitable for a Princess."

"That, sir, I consider a compliment," Vanda smiled, "and I only hope that I can live up to the part you have created for me. It will be terrible if I make any mistakes."

"The first point is that Charles and I have to treat you with great respect and not forget to say, *ma'am*, every other word."

Vanda laughed.

"Charles will not like it – he is more used to saying I am a silly little idiot or ruffling my hair with his hand."

The Earl gave an exclamation of mock dismay.

"We have to be careful, all of us," he cautioned. "You will find your Ladies-in-Waiting very self-effacing and they will only appear when you want them."

Dinner was served and as soon as it was finished the Earl left them.

Despite the fact that Irene worried him by being so indiscreet, he still found her alluring.

She greeted the Earl wearing a diaphanous gown which revealed more of her perfect figure than it concealed.

He found it impossible not to respond to her passionate kisses and she lured him artfully into her bedroom almost before he was aware of it.

It was some hours later before the Earl said somewhat sleepily,

"I ought to be going home. You know as well as I do that the servants will talk if I stay too late."

Irene laughed and it was a very pretty sound.

"They are too frightened of me to talk about us," she answered.

"You can never be certain and just in case your husband returns from Windsor earlier than you expect, I will not be dining with you tomorrow night. Actually I am going abroad."

"Going abroad!" Irene cried and now her voice was sharp.

"Only for a short while, but I need to approve some innovations on my father's yacht and the Captain insists on running it across the Channel before we pay a very large bill for the alterations."

"But surely you can do that on Friday night after Arthur has returned," Irene pouted petulantly.

"I did suggest it, but unfortunately the man who installed them and who of course has to be on board, has another engagement."

Irene put her arms around him.

"I cannot let you go Favin," she purred. "You know how precious the few hours we spend together are and I want you to be with me tomorrow night."

"As I want to be with you, but alas, my dear, it is impossible."

"Nothing is impossible and if the worst comes to the worst I will come with you on your yacht."

"That is something you cannot do," he frowned. "You know as well as I do that someone will find out and it will cause a scandal."

"Why should anyone find out?"

"Because, my dear, you are very beautiful and people talk. No one is going to believe that you are on board my yacht simply because you like the sea and are interested in new gadgets."

Irene drew closer to him.

"Please stay with me, darling," she begged. "It is Heaven to be in your arms and I love you more than I have ever loved any man."

The Earl did not answer and after a moment she said,

"If I were free, do you swear that you would marry me?"

"The question does not arise. Your husband is very much alive and there is no doubt that he will live for many more years."

"We cannot be certain," Irene said almost beneath her breath.

Then as if she had suddenly thought of it, she asked,

"You are not taking anyone else with you on your yacht?"

"Only a friend of mine who is as interested in machinery as I am."

"If I thought it was a woman, I would kill her," Irene hissed. "If you look at any woman except me, she will die, and that is something you are never to forget."

"I think you are talking nonsense. As you well know, there is no other woman in my life, nor is there likely to be. You are underestimating your own beauty and your own charm, Irene."

"I love you so completely and absolutely that it is impossible to live without you," Irene sighed passionately.

She kissed his shoulder before saying,

"We have to be together. We were meant for each other and it is only by the cruelty of fate that I am already married."

"But you are," the Earl pointed out again, "and therefore there is nothing we can do about it."

"I can think of quite a number of things," Irene answered slowly. "And when I am your wife, I shall be the happiest woman in the world!"

She spoke as if every word was the truth.

Yet the Earl could not help thinking her words would not have been said if there had not been a Ducal coronet behind his head.

"You are depressing me," he remarked aloud. "Let us enjoy ourselves while we can and not worry about tomorrow."

"But I shall worry because you are going away and I shall be counting every moment until you return."

"I will not be too long, but you must know what it

means to install all the latest innovations into an old yacht. It always takes longer than one expects."

"If it takes any longer than I can stand," Irene said, "I shall come and join you wherever you are. Promise you will write to me every day and tell me where I can get in touch with you."

"I am not certain myself, but I will certainly do my best."

He did not want to talk anymore, feeling he was on very dangerous ground.

He therefore kissed Irene until she forgot everything but the fire and excitement of their passion.

It was just two hours later as the Earl climbed wearily into his own bed at Brackenshaw House that he remembered Irene's threats which he thought were absurd and unrestrained.

He had always disliked hysterical women and they had tried many times to tie themselves to him so that there was no escape.

At least, he thought with satisfaction, that it was impossible for Irene to join him or to correspond with him once he was on his way to Beirut.

He had already told Charles that he had sent a messenger on ahead.

The man had left this morning with a letter for Sheik Abu Hamid. In it the Earl had informed him that he was leaving on his yacht for Beirut the following day.

He was bringing with him Princess Vanda of Thessaly who is, as the Sheik would doubtless remember, the daughter of the late Prince Nikos and Princess Louise, a cousin of Her Majesty Queen Victoria.

He had arranged, he wrote in his letter, for the Princess to be accompanied by two English Ladies-in-Waiting, while she was on board the *Sea Serpent*.

But he considered it would be advisable for her to be waited on by two Syrian women on her arrival. He knew that the Sheik could easily provide them.

'If your people are meeting us at Beirut,' the Earl wrote, *'I hope you will be kind enough to equip them with horses which Her Royal Highness and I, and my friend Captain Charles Kenwood, can ride.*

It is something we are all looking forward to and who could provide us with better horses than Your Highness.'

He signed himself with a fulsome appreciation of the Sheik's hospitality, adding that Her Royal Highness was very interested in his horses.

Also not having visited any part of the Middle East before, she was looking forward to viewing his countryside. When the Earl had finished the letter, he was pleased with what he had written.

He had not told the Sheik anything personal about the Royal visitor as it would make him curious.

He would also find it difficult to discover anything about her.

All that mattered was that the visit would go off well and then he and Charles would be able to obtain the horses they desired.

It all seemed, the Earl thought, to be going too smoothly to be true.

To himself he repeated the most common saying in Arab lands, *'Insh Allah.'*

This means quite simply, *'God has willed it so.'*

*

It was a bright sunny day when they set off in the Earl's comfortable London carriage from Brackenshaw House. Following them was a brake conveying their luggage and the Earl's valet who had been with him for many years.

Carstairs had travelled with him whenever he journeyed abroad and he was not surprised when the Earl told him he was returning to Syria.

"I thinks as you wouldn't be able to leave them 'orses alone, my Lord," he said.

"I want them desperately, Carstairs and Captain Kenwood needs them too."

"A good deal more than you do, my Lord, from what I 'ears," Carstairs answered.

"What have you heard?"

"That the Captain's having difficulty in making ends meet and that be nothin' new!"

The Earl had travelled alone with Carstairs for so many years and he recognised that the older man looked after him as if he was still a boy.

He always talked to him frankly as he would not have talked to any other servant.

'It is rather like having a nanny,' he thought.

Carstairs was overwhelmed by Vanda when he met her.

"That be the prettiest lady that has come inside this 'ouse ever since I've been 'ere," he said to his Master. "Seems a pity there's no more like her."

"What is wrong with those who have come earlier?" the Earl asked.

Carstairs's opinion on people always amused him.

"If you be speakin' of her Ladyship, I wouldn't trust her an inch further than I can see her. Beautiful she may be. At the same time she's too pushy for my likin', and her stops at nothin' to get her own way."

This was indeed something that the Earl had already found.

It was of comfort to know that Carstairs was not deceived by Irene's 'honeyed tongue' as he called it.

"She says one thing and thinks another," Carstairs rambled on. "From what I makes out all the servants in his Lordship's house be frightened to death of her."

"Why should they be?" the Earl wanted to know.

He knew it was bad form to talk of other people's servants, but with Carstairs it was different. He had got him out of a lot of trouble one way and another.

"I warned you before, my Lord," Carstairs answered, "and I'm warnin' you now, that Lady won't do you no good and the sooner you be rid of her the better!"

The Earl laughed but he did not answer.

He was aware that Carstairs was brave enough to say what he was thinking himself.

*

They joined the *Sea Serpent* a little way down the Thames from the House of Lords.

The engines began to turn and the Earl was thinking with relief that the yacht was carrying him far away from Irene.

He even hoped against hope that she would forget him, but felt it was unlikely, but because she was so attractive there would be a number of men only too willing to take his place.

But he had an uneasy feeling that she would wait for his return and would pounce on him once again before he could escape.

At least for the moment he had secured some breathing space.

He told himself hopefully that something might turn up in his absence, although somewhat cynically a part of his brain was telling him that prospective Dukes were few and far between.

Although she undoubtedly desired him as a man, Irene was also insatiably ambitious and of course she wanted to end up a Duchess and to wear the Brackenshaw jewels.

It would make her the winner in the most testing social race ever run.

The *Sea Serpent* was now moving down the river and the Earl felt he was on his way to freedom.

He was leaving Irene behind.

He could only pray that she would forget him and he wanted to forget everything she had said to him last night.

'It was just hysterical talk,' he told himself.

Vanda, who had seen her luggage taken into a very attractive cabin, came running up on deck and joined the Earl who was standing at the rails.

He was watching the Houses of Parliament fade into the distance.

"We are moving!" she cried. "We are leaving England and I still cannot believe I am not dreaming!"

"You must wake up, because we have quite a long way to go," the Earl replied.

"It cannot be too long for me and you know how wonderful it will be for Charles to be seeing, even if he cannot buy them, the wonderful Arab horses you have told me about."

"He will enjoy them as much as I do," the Earl replied.

"But I want to thank you for including him in your enterprise. It is very, very kind of you and it is the most marvellous thing that has ever happened to me."

"Perhaps when we arrive you may find it all disappointing."

"That will be impossible. If Charles is interested in Arab horses so am I. After all they are very much part of English history and it is only right that they should be winning our races as they did when the Roman Emperor Severus held races in Yorkshire."

The Earl looked at her in surprise.

"How did you know that?"

"Strangely enough, I was reading about it only a month or so ago, Severus organised races with real Arabs early in the third century AD."

The Earl was amused.

He was not used to women who talked about Roman Emperors when they might have been talking about him.

"What else do you know about Arab horses?" he enquired.

"So much I can hardly tell you in a few minutes," Vanda replied. "But I expect you know that Henry VIII took a personal interest in breeding from Eastern sires, and Cardinal Wolsey was so keen on horses with Eastern blood that he took for himself an Arab stallion which had been sent to the King by the Duke of Urbino."

"Now you are making me very interested. I suppose I must have heard these stories before, but I had forgotten them."

"Then it is time you and Charles learned all about them again," Vanda said almost severely. "There is quite a bit in the history books about the Norman horses at the Battle of Hastings being much lighter, because they had Arab blood in them, than the heavy stallions which had been imported from Flanders by King Harold."

"Now I know I am back at school," the Earl professed. "And I have the uncomfortable feeling that I am at the bottom of the class!"

Charles joined them and he remarked,

"Her Royal Highness is taking me to task for being an ignoramus."

For a moment Charles looked at him in surprise before remembering their plan of action that Vanda was to be 'Her Royal Highness' from the moment they left Park Lane.

"I am sure that it is very clever of Her Royal Highness," he said after a pause. "But surely she is not telling you, my Lord, anything you did not know already."

"I am trying to pretend I had long forgotten it."

Charles laughed.

"You will have to be up early if you are going to get the better of Van- I mean Her Royal Highness. She has read ever book in our library and I am quite certain she will read every one in yours."

"I do hope you have brought some books on board," Vanda enquired.

"I do not think you will be disappointed in the books you will find on the bookshelves in the cabin I use as my study," the Earl responded. "My father never thought of such a thing, but I decided, if I was to be at sea for any length of time, I not only needed books but somewhere comfortable to write. So this is perhaps the only yacht which has a cabin which is not for sleeping but for reading."

Vanda laughed.

"I think that is a wonderful idea! I was only thinking when I looked over my luggage this morning that we might have spent a little time in a bookshop."

"We have spent quite enough money," Charles intervened sharply, "and I was only thinking after I went to bed that what we have forgotten is white gloves which you will be expected to wear on every formal occasion."

"Once again I go to the top of the class. I packed at

least six pairs of Mama's and I cannot believe, whatever you say, that I have to wear white gloves all the time in the desert!"

"They are worn only on formal occasions," the Earl advised gravely, "and anything you have forgotten we can always buy in any port where we stop."

Vanda smiled at him.

"You really are a magician. You have waved your magic wand and Charles and I are here in a dream boat on the way to a magical Kingdom where I am quite certain even the horses have wings."

The Earl laughed.

"I only hope you will not be disappointed."

"How could I be? And please, before we do anything else, can we explore your wonderful yacht? And could you show me all the improvements Charles tells me you have made."

"I should very much like to do that."

Then Vanda looked over her shoulder as if to see that no one was listening.

"I think," she said in a low voice, "if the Princess was behaving properly, she would ask to be introduced to the crew."

"You are quite right," Charles jumped in before the Earl could speak. "That is one up to Her Royal Highness and do not forget it."

"I will not do so and I am extremely impressed," the Earl admitted.

The way he spoke seemed very funny to Vanda and they were all three laughing as they moved towards the bridge.

CHAPTER FOUR

Vanda was introduced to the crew as they moved around the yacht. They all seemed pleased when she shook them by the hand and told them how interested she was in what they were doing.

The two women who were to be her Ladies-in-Waiting curtsied correctly and looked relieved when Vanda told them that she hoped she would not need them very often on the voyage.

"I am having a complete holiday," she confided, "because I have had a very difficult time lately at home and I need to rest."

Everyone thought this was a good idea.

Vanda only hoped, when they laughed so much at dinner, that they did not think she had been making a mountain out of a molehill.

The sea was, as usual, very rough in the Bay of Biscay and luckily Vanda had always believed that she was a good sailor. She proved it by not feeling the least seasick, but she did hear that the Steward's wife had taken to her berth.

Vanda was in fact so thrilled by everything that was happening to her and even the waves towering over the bow of the yacht were an irrepressible delight.

The Earl thought that no one could be more charming or easier to entertain. If Vanda was not talking and laughing with him and her brother, she was reading.

She was very pleased with the books she found in his study and she found one volume on horses which contained a long dissertation on the Arab breed.

When they stopped at Gibraltar, the Earl went ashore and bought Vanda a beautiful Chinese shawl embroidered with flowers.

She was charmed with his present and claimed she had never owned anything so beautiful.

"You are so kind," she enthused, "and you have already spent so much money on my clothes."

"That was business," the Earl replied. "What I have given you now is pleasure."

She smiled at him.

He thought that no one could be more unselfconscious than Vanda about her looks.

He was so used to women always fussing about themselves, if they were sitting in the sun, if the wind was blowing their hair or if they were disarranged in any way.

None of this seemed to bother Vanda at all. It did not occur to her she should do anything about her looks.

She was up early in the morning and on deck, fascinated either by the sea or any land they were passing.

When they reached Malta she did not feel like going ashore. The Earl had rather expected her to go shopping, but she stayed happily on board until they set sail again.

*

The Earl, before he left, had been forced to tell his secretary the truth about his intentions.

"I am going to be away for quite a long time, Wilson, but you have to assure anyone who enquires for me that you expect me back in a week or so."

He saw by the expression on the secretary's face that he realised he was in an oblique way referring to Lady Grantham.

"I do not want any letters sent after me," the Earl ordered, "and they must await my return. Except that you must inform me if anything important happens in the family."

He was of course referring to his father's health, although there was no reason to think that the Duke would die in the next month or so.

"If there is anything really important you can send me a letter to Beirut by special messenger and I will doubtless receive it in a few days. Equally I do not wish to receive any communications unless they are absolutely necessary."

"I understand my Lord," Mr. Wilson replied, "and I will be as tactful as possible with those who make enquiries about your return."

The Earl understood without putting it any more clearly that he would deal with Irene. He had sighed with relief as he left the secretary's office.

*

There were fortunately no letters waiting for him either at Gibraltar or Malta, so they sailed on as quickly as possible to Athens.

The Earl had thoughts of stopping at Rome, but that would entail a long diversion from the direct route, and he was in a hurry to reach Beirut.

For the first time since she had come aboard, Vanda longed to go ashore at Athens as she had always been fascinated by Greek history, and she wanted to visit the places she had read about and of course to see the statues of the Goddesses.

"What I would really like," she sighed as they left Malta, "is to visit Delphi."

"You will have to go there on your honeymoon," the Earl responded. "I have always thought it a special place for honeymooners as the Gods from Olympus bless those who visit them."

"What a lovely idea! If and when I have a honeymoon, I shall insist that it is where my husband takes me."

"The man may not be able to afford it," Charles objected.

"We shall make so much money with your Arab horses that you will be able to give me my honeymoon as a wedding present!" Vanda quipped.

"Even so it would be much too expensive," Charles protested. "But do not count your chickens before they are hatched, you have not found yourself a husband."

"I have not yet had the chance to look very far for one."

"When we return to England," the Earl suggested, "you and Charles must come and stay at Brackenshaw House and you shall meet all the eligible young men in London. I promise that you will be a huge success."

Vanda clapped her hands.

"You are the kindest man who ever existed and I only hope the Arab horses come up to your expectations. If they do not, you will just have to say that you cannot afford them."

The Earl smiled.

"That is a promise," he said, "and I shall not forget about it."

He thought as he spoke how furious Irene would be if he invited anyone as beautiful as Vanda to his London house. It would be impossible for her not to be jealous.

Vanda was not only much younger than Irene, she was

at the same time so uniquely and serenely beautiful.

Every day the Earl thought Vanda looked more exquisite than she had the day before.

It seemed to him extraordinary that, even living in the country, no man had so far discovered her.

'I will certainly,' he told himself, 'do everything I can for her on my return. No one could be more accommodating than she has been and she is playing her part splendidly.'

When the Stewards were attending them, Vanda was always at her most formal and the Earl and Charles both remembered to say 'ma'am'.

Only when they were alone did Charles tease her as he had always done ever since she was a child, but she answered him back in a humorous manner which kept them all laughing.

As they passed the Greek islands, Vanda looked at them wistfully and the Earl was aware that she was longing to stop and visit Delos where Apollo had been born.

But she did not plead with him to do anything he did not wish to do and so they passed on quickly towards Beirut.

When they sailed into port and saw the City which was built right on the sea line, the sun was shining.

"Now," he told Vanda, "your real ordeal begins. I have notified the Sheik of your arrival and the party who will escort us to his house will be waiting for us on the quay."

"I must look my best and I cannot tell you how much I appreciate the beautiful clothes you have given me."

"You do indeed look very lovely in them."

She smiled at the Earl.

"Do you mean that or is it just a *façon de parler*, as the French would say?"

"I do mean it," he said. "In fact a great number of

people will tell you in the future, Vanda, that you are very beautiful."

She looked at him in surprise. It had never really crossed her mind that she was beautiful.

The Earl thought that a hundred men would tell her how gorgeous she was once she appeared in London. With her golden hair and her perfect complexion, she was in fact exactly what one expected and hoped for in an English beauty.

But it was Vanda's eyes which made her different from any woman he had ever seen.

He thought now as they lit up that she was as exceptional as the Arab horses. Perhaps a better image was a jewel of great value.

The Earl had been right and waiting on the quay were a number of Arabs sent by the Sheik.

They all bowed low on being introduced to the Princess and then they were escorted to the most important hotel in Beirut, where they explained to the Earl that after food and a rest, it was arranged that they should ride to the Sheik's residence.

Vanda was delighted.

She thought however it would have been more convenient if they had known before they left the yacht that they were to ride to the Sheik's residence.

She changed into a riding habit with the help of the two Ladies-in-Waiting who had come ashore with her. They were about to go back to the yacht, but the Earl had insisted that they were seen to be in attendance.

The Arab in charge of the welcoming party took him on one side. He told the Earl that the women who would look after Her Royal Highness when they arrived had not been brought with them, as they thought it would be too hard a journey for them.

He was well aware that English women were good riders and could spend a long day in the saddle.

"But our women," he said, "prefer to stay at home and wait for the return of the menfolk."

"I understand," the Earl replied, "and her Royal Highness will be quite safe in your protection until we arrive at the Sheik's house."

It was not yet noon when they set off on the magnificent Arab stallions which were provided by their escort and the Earl and Charles were delighted with them.

Vanda was so thrilled she ran out of adjectives to say how much she admired them.

As they rode through the city the Earl thought no one could have looked more attractive on horseback or, in fact, so Royal.

Vanda rode ahead as if it was her right and the two Englishmen kept respectfully behind her.

There was only one matter which had upset the Earl and that was when they had reached Beirut, he was handed a letter from his secretary which had arrived only the day before they docked.

He suspected that it must be bad news after his instructions to Mr. Wilson and therefore he did not open the letter immediately, as all the time they were surrounded by the Arabs until they set off for their host's house.

He told himself that he would read it when they arrived and then it would not be his fault if there was a delay in sending an answer.

Once they were outside the City the land began to look more like a desert. There were just a few trees and a little fertile country before they reached the sand.

Their cavalcade of nearly fifteen aroused a good deal of interest and people waved to them from the streets.

Vanda, as if she was as important as they thought her to be, gave them a little nod, occasionally raising her hand to respond to their waving arms.

She thought no one could have been accompanied by a more dramatic escort.

The beautiful Arab stallions they were riding might have stepped out of a picture and the Arabs wearing their black and white robes looked almost majestic.

After they had been riding for two hours, Vanda understood why they had been given something to eat and drink before they left.

The suitcases which contained the clothes they had just taken off were following them on slower horses and the luggage which came from the yacht had, she was told, already gone ahead.

Their horses were built for speed and Vanda realised she had never ridden as fast as she was able to do now.

She had always been told that Arab horses were famous for their endurance and later in the afternoon she was beginning to feel tried.

She felt somewhat ashamed when her horse did not seem to feel any fatigue, as even though they had been galloping for what seemed like hours, it was still comparatively fresh.

It was four o'clock in the afternoon before the Arab who was riding beside Vanda pointed into the distance.

They had been in wholly desert country for the last three hours but now there were some mountains in view in the distance.

Then, as one of the Arabs pointed, Vanda saw what appeared to her to be a clump of trees in the centre of which loomed a large house.

It was impossible to see very clearly but she felt that it

must be the Sheik's. It was built low like all Eastern houses, but was obviously impressive.

A number of roofs could be seen behind the house surrounded by what seemed to be fertile ground, and Vanda realised at once that the houses were built in the middle of an oasis which would keep them well supplied with water.

She thought the oasis itself was most picturesque with its trees and vegetation after the dusty desert and was certainly made even more so by the nearness of the mountains.

She could understand why the Sheik had built a house in that particular place so far away from civilisation.

It was then that Vanda turned to the Earl,

"I forgot to ask, how do we address our hosts?"

"If he is a Ruler as ours is, you say 'Your Highness' otherwise, 'Your Excellency.'"

As they drew nearer the Arabs began to move even faster as their horses knew they were home and they too were very willing to quicken their pace. They galloped towards the house at what seemed to Vanda to be an almost superhuman speed.

They swept in through the trees to halt at an imposing entrance to what was clearly a very fine Eastern building.

Even as they arrived she could see a man in pure white robes waiting for them.

This must be the Sheik Abu Hamid.

The Arabs pulled in their horses abruptly so that they seemed to genuflect to him with their legs in respect.

Vanda rode forward until she was almost level with the Sheik and a servant helped her down from her mount.

The Sheik stepped forward to greet them in quite good English,

"I welcome Your Royal Highness to my humble home,

and it is with the greatest pleasure I offer you a salutation from my people."

"I am very delighted to be here, Your Highness," Vanda replied.

The two men joined her and the Earl shook the Sheik by the hand and introduced Charles to him.

They were taken into a large room furnished with soft low sofas on which they were expected to sit.

Coffee was brought in immediately together with some delicious sweetmeats made from nuts and honey.

Vanda was hungry after her long ride and enjoyed them.

Then the Earl suggested that Her Royal Highness should take a rest before dinner.

The Sheik clapped his hands and instantly two Bedouin women appeared who were introduced to Vanda as her Ladies-in-Waiting. She found, although they could not speak English, they were both fairly fluent in French.

They escorted her down some long passages to what they told her was a room specifically arranged in a European fashion so that she could feel at home.

It did not in fact look very European to Vanda.

There was a low bed on a platform about a foot high and what she realised was a dressing table with a golden-framed mirror in the centre of it.

She said of course how much she appreciated her room.

The women bowed and almost prostrated themselves in front of her.

Her luggage had not yet arrived from the yacht so Vanda undressed and lay down on the bed wearing only her chemise and a petticoat.

The two women asked if she would like them to stay

in the room. She thanked them for their kindness and she said in French that she preferred to be alone as she was a very light sleeper.

Once they had left she got out of bed and ran to the window as she realised that darkness came quickly in the East and she wanted to take a last look at her surroundings.

Now she could see a number of horses which were being brought into a sort of enclosure before it was dark. Even though they were at some distance, she could see how magnificent they were.

She appreciated how important it was for the Earl and Charles to be able to buy them at reasonable prices.

'We have done it!' she thought. 'We have made it here and so far we have been very, very lucky.'

*

In another room, actually not far from Vanda's, the Earl was opening the letter which he had brought with him from Beirut.

It contained an enclosure on very familiar sky blue writing-paper.

Mr. Wilson's letter was explanatory,

'*My Lord,*

You may think it unnecessary for me to disturb you so early in your journey, but Lady Grantham called after you had left and made such a terrible scene about getting in touch with you that I had to promise I would send you the enclosed letter.

Her ladyship behaved in such a strange manner I was afraid that if I did not do as she asked, she would bring other people to convince me that the letter she wished you to receive must in some way reach you.

I only hope it will not disturb your Lordship but I feel her Ladyship will not be satisfied until she has an answer.

I remain

Yours respectfully

Basil Wilson.'

The Earl read the letter again and his lips set in a straight line. The last thing he wanted was Irene making a scene in front of his servants.

He had known before he left England that she would be furious if she knew he was to be away for long and he could only wonder why she had acted more quickly than he anticipated.

He opened her letter.

As he read the first words he knew what to expect.

She accused him first of being a liar, a hypocrite, a deceiver and then as he read on she wrote,

'*You swore to me that there was no one going with you on this journey except a man.*

Edward's friend, Lord Mayfield, told him that when he was going to the House of Lords, he saw you boarding your yacht a little lower down the Thames.

He had in fact admired the yacht when it was anchored there and was interested to see you going aboard with two friends, a man and a woman.'

She carried on upbraiding him even more angrily than she had already done.

If he was prepared to take a woman with him, why had he not taken her?

'*If she is someone you are interested in and whom you care for more than me, I swear I will kill her.*

You are mine, Favin, mine completely, and I will not permit any woman to take you from me.'

She scrawled her name and like her writing it was almost indecipherable.

The Earl reckoned that she must have been completely hysterical when she wrote the letter.

There was nothing he could do.

He tore it up into such small pieces that it would be impossible for anyone, even if they were interested, to put it together.

There was no reason to be afraid of what Irene or the London gossips could do to him at this moment.

They were a long way from England, but he was taking no chances.

'Why did I ever become involved with anyone who behaves in such a ridiculous manner?' he asked himself.

Then he recognised that if the truth was to be told, he never wanted to see Irene again.

She attracted him physically, of course she did, which was not surprising considering how beautiful she is and their passion together had been abnormally tempestuous.

He felt now that it was something which made him feel embarrassed. He did not want to think about her and he certainly did not want to have anything more to do with Irene.

At the same time he was very conscious that she would be waiting for him on his return.

She might even try in some way to hurt Vanda although he could not really believe that she would go to such extremes.

On the other hand, who could control a woman who could not control herself?

The Earl rose from where he was sitting to walk to the window as Vanda had done in her room.

He looked out and by now it was nearly dark.

The first stars were beginning to gleam and there was an irresistible beauty about the skyline.

It made him feel that anything which happened elsewhere was irrelevant and unimportant and yet he knew he must not underestimate the harm which Irene could do to him. A scandal such as she might create would horrify and disgust his family and friends.

'Whatever can I do?' he muttered to himself.

But there was no answer.

Only the growing darkness of the night and the stars overhead seemed to tell him that the world was a large place and a jealous woman a very small part of it, but he was still feeling apprehensive.

*

It was thus a relief when he changed for dinner and went to join the Sheik. He found Vanda already there talking animatedly to their host.

They were speaking half in English and half in French, in which, the Earl realised, she was most proficient.

She gave him a smile when he entered the room.

He bowed to her as to Royalty and she graciously inclined her head.

"His Highness has been telling me about his wonderful horses," she told the Earl. "And tomorrow we are to have a special demonstration by his tribe which I shall find most enthralling."

"So shall I," the Earl agreed. "It is an event I have seen only once before, and I can assure Your Royal Highness that it is a thrilling spectacle."

The Sheik was obviously gratified by what they were saying.

When Charles came in the conversation was all about horses and how the Sheik himself had built up one of the finest breeds in the whole of the Middle East.

"My stable has cost me a great deal of money," he

confessed, "But it has also given me more enjoyment than I have ever experienced. What man could ask for more?"

"What indeed?" the Earl replied impressed.

Vanda wondered if there were any women in the Sheik's house and she felt certain that he must keep a harem somewhere.

Her two Bedouin Ladies-in-Waiting were, she thought, over thirty and they were beginning to show their age as women invariably did in the East, but they must have been pretty once – perhaps when they had first arrived in the desert it was to join the Sheik's harem.

There was no one at dinner except the three of them and their host. The food was delicious and so was the first drink which was offered to Vanda.

The men drank wine which was a considerable concession to them as Europeans.

Fortunately Vanda had learned when they were on the yacht how the Bedouins ate and she was therefore not dismayed when she realised there were no knives, forks or spoons.

The main dish was lamb.

She knew, because the Earl had told her, that it was cooked in camel's milk and *burgoul,* which is wheat boiled in butter or oil and dried in the sun. The wheat is then pressed for a year.

Vanda did not find it difficult to shape the lamb into small pieces with the *burgoul.*

She then put it gingerly into her mouth.

She had to be careful because the Earl had warned her that the food was always very hot and it needed care not to burn her fingers let alone her mouth.

Because she was hungry, Vanda thought food had never tasted better.

She also enjoyed the freshly baked bread called *jusri* and there were several other dishes which were made of strange ingredients she had never tasted.

To finish the meal there was *henreyne*, a delicious sweetmeat made of bread, butter and dates all blended together.

Vanda guessed that they were being waited on by slaves and she was glad when one of them brought her a basin to wash her hands after she had finished eating.

The Sheik talked very little whilst dinner was being served.

Finally when they were brought coffee, he smiled at Vanda and said,

"I hope Your Royal Highness is not too tired?"

"I was a little tired when we arrived, but after such a delicious dinner I feel rested and ready to admire everything that Your Highness plans to show us."

"That is just what I hoped you would say," the Sheik commented.

He clapped his hands.

A curtain was drawn back at the end of the room to the sound of Arab music. Four very pretty women appeared, elaborately dressed in jewels and gowns which shimmered with every movement they made.

They performed a gyrating dance Vanda reckoned was called 'belly dancing.' Her father had described it to her as he had seen it in Egypt and a great number of other places in the East.

She was fascinated, as she thought her two companions must be.

The women undoubtedly danced extremely well and when they had finished they bowed deeply to their audience.

"That was most interesting, Your Highness," Vanda

said appreciatively. "Thank you so much for showing us your beautiful Eastern dancing."

"I believed it would amuse Your Royal Highness," the Sheik replied.

Although it was not late, he obviously expected her to retire so she rose to her feet saying that she was tired and that she hoped she would be able to ride early in the morning.

"I will arrange everything," the Sheik promised.

He bent over her hand, although he did not kiss it, but to Vanda's surprise the Earl actually touched her skin with his lips.

"You have been magnificent," he whispered so that only she could hear.

She smiled at him before she turned away.

She walked with the two Bedouin women towards her bedroom. She thought as she did so that it had been a very fascinating and unusual evening.

'It was wonderful of the Earl to ask me to come,' she told herself.

Then she wondered if, now she had left, the Sheik would introduce the Earl and Charles to some of his attractive harem.

She did not know why, but she felt a little pang of resentment. It was just in case the Earl admired the women who had been dancing or others like them, more than her.

When she had dined on the yacht wearing one of her new evening gowns, she sensed that he was admiring her.

He had not said much, although Charles remarked on her gown saying,

"You look tip-top in that dress."

On another night he had said,

"I knew as soon as I saw that gown, you would look fantastic in it. It really is a winner."

81

Vanda had looked at the Earl hoping for his approval.

After all, she thought, her gown had cost him a lot of money, but he had said the expense was unimportant beside the horses.

Yet she wanted him to feel that his pounds had been well spent and she had been sure that he had looked at her with admiration.

On most nights he had only lifted his glass and said,

"To Your Royal Highness."

On another occasion he had remarked,

"Vanda, you look Royal in every sense of the word."

She was not sure whether his comment was a compliment or not, but she hoped that he meant it.

Now the Bedouin women who had helped her undress had left her alone, so she pulled back the curtains.

The stars filled the sky and the moon seemed larger than any moon she had ever seen. It lit up the desert with its silver light and it was so lovely that Vanda just stood there for a long time.

The scene was something she had never seen before and once they had left she would never see it again.

Then instinctively she wished there was someone with her and they could gaze at the stars together.

She understood that the stars meant something very precious to those who lived under them like the desert Arabs.

The gypsies who came from the East always believed that each man possessed a star of his own in the sky.

Vanda hoped that she owned one.

But she thought it was unlikely in this part of the world where women were unimportant and so she could not expect to be privileged.

She sent a prayer up to the sky that one day she would

find love and that the man she loved would kiss her under the stars and make the beauty of them even more wonderful than they were at this moment.

'Who could not feel love where there is so much beauty?' she asked herself.

She closed the curtains over the windows and went back to bed.

CHAPTER FIVE

Vanda was having breakfast waited on by her two Bedouin Ladies-in-Waiting.

She was not quite certain how the timetable for today would be organised so she asked one of them to find out.

She had slept well and when she climbed out of bed, she put on one of the pretty nightgowns she had made herself.

Her dressing gown had belonged to her mother. It was really more of a negligee, made of blue satin trimmed with rows of lace and it fastened at the neck with a little bow of velvet in the same colour with velvet bows all down the front.

Vanda had not yet arranged her hair and it was falling in cascades over her shoulders.

The Lady-in-Waiting reappeared accompanied by the Earl much to Vanda's surprise.

He made his Royal obeisance at the door which Vanda acknowledged seated on a sofa with a low table in front of her.

"Good morning, my Lord," she greeted him. "I was wondering about our programme for today."

The Earl was standing in front of her and after a moment she remembered she had to tell him to sit down.

"Please be seated, my Lord, being so tall you are somewhat overpowering."

The Earl gave a laugh and replied,

"Thank you, ma'am, it is most considerate of you."

He sat down on a sofa and said,

"I have arranged with our host that we should go to inspect his horses as soon as you are ready. As they are a little way from here we will of course be riding."

Vanda gave a cry of delight.

"Tomorrow," he continued, "a spectacular party is being given for you. The Sheik has invited all the other tribes in the neighbourhood to see the parade of his horses, and of course their leaders will have the honour of being presented to Your Royal Highness."

The Earl's eyes were twinkling.

Vanda was aware that he was amused at the idea of her being so important. However she was determined to behave properly in front of her Bedouin Ladies-in-Waiting and she therefore answered,

"Thank you, my Lord, for this information. I will dress immediately I have finished my breakfast and join you."

The Earl knew that he was now dismissed.

Rising before he gave the Royal bow he added,

"Your Royal Highness is most gracious."

He left the room and Vanda excitedly ran to her bedroom.

She was not certain from what he had said whether tomorrow she would be wearing a riding habit or a dress. She therefore chose for today the habit she thought was less spectacular.

It was however very smart, made in blue *piqué* which had just become popular in France and decorated with white braid. There was a little muslin blouse inset with lace to wear under it and beneath the full skirt there was a petticoat also trimmed with lace.

Fortunately when she was choosing her hats Vanda had not forgotten those she would wear with her riding habits. It was, although she was unaware of it, a fashion which had been introduced by the '*Pretty Horsebreakers.*'

Her chosen hat boasted a tall round crown surmounted with chiffon and the two ends floated out at the back.

It was extremely becoming.

When Vanda appeared to find the Sheik and the two gentlemen waiting for her, she knew they all looked at her admiringly.

The Sheik bowed over her hand saying,

"Your Royal Highness is as beautiful as the flowers in my garden and the birds flying in the sky. I kneel at your feet in admiration."

He spoke in a mixture of England and French.

Vanda thought his praise was very touching so she thanked him profusely.

Then her eyes lit up as three horses were brought to the front of the house.

They were all exceptionally fine Arabs.

The three men rode stallions while she was mounted on a very beautiful mare.

They rode North-Eastwards and Vanda was informed that this part of the desert was called El Hammad.

The sun was shining but it was not too hot and the horses were obviously longing for exercise.

They rode for nearly half-an-hour at a tremendous pace and then Vanda saw ahead of her what looked like a high black rock. For a moment she could not think what it was.

As they drew nearer she realised that it was a number of black tents all pitched close together on a piece of ground which appeared to be very fertile.

As they drew nearer still she could see the horses waiting for them and there were to her delight well over a hundred.

The Sheik's tribesmen raised their arms in salute as she approached.

Horses were moving about loose, apparently finding something to eat beneath their feet, whilst others were being ridden by the tribesmen. Each one seemed to Vanda finer and more spirited than the last.

The horses were brought up for them to inspect.

Both the Earl and Charles were finding it impossible to decide which ones they wanted most, as every horse they saw was so fine and perfect to look at.

The tribesmen were only too willing to extol the virtues of their horses and for some time no one paid much attention to Vanda, who moved around patting one horse after another.

She guessed the reason why her brother and the Earl were talking so intently to the Sheik. They were obviously trying to persuade him to part with the horses they particularly desired.

Soon after noon the Sheik insisted on taking them into a large tent where luncheon was waiting for them and it was very different from the fare they had been offered the night before.

They were served with what Vanda recognised as a favourite food of the Arabs called *kemmáye* which is a kind of truffle grown in the desert.

Vanda exclaimed that she found it most delectable as the Sheik explained it closely resembled the true truffle which the French prized so highly.

"We have three different species here," he informed her, "the red, the black and the white."

Kemmáye is boiled in milk until it forms a paste over which melted butter has been poured.

Vanda had tasted hers rather tentatively at first, but found it was very pleasant to eat.

The Earl pointed out that it was a 'convenient' food as it was available in the most remote spots in the desert.

There were also small quails eggs and plenty of the fresh baked *fisre* with plenty of butter.

When they had finished eating the Sheik proposed,

"Now I suggest we all rest. It is very hot at this time of day and afterwards my men wish to give Your Royal Highness a demonstration of their riding."

There was nothing his English guests could do but agree.

Vanda was taken into a small tent where there were two Bedouin women on hand to help her take off her riding habit.

She then lay on an Eastern bed and the women left her alone. She had the idea however that one of them had sat down outside the door just in case she needed her.

Although she had slept well the night before, to her surprise she fell fast asleep.

When she woke it was because the two women had returned, waiting to help her back into her riding habit.

When she walked out into the sun, she found Charles and the Earl with the Sheik.

They sat down in what seemed to be a kind of Royal Box specially built for the occasion. It was raised from the ground with three comfortable seats inside.

For a moment there appeared to be no horses within sight and then there was a shot far away in the distance followed by another.

A few seconds later Vanda could see men galloping towards them at full speed. They were firing as they did so, yelling and hanging over their horses' necks with their bridles in their teeth, waving long feathered lances in the air. They threw up their lances and then caught them again at full gallop.

She remembered reading about the wild plunging charge of the Bedouin horsemen, but Vanda had never imagined it was quite so fantastic or so exhilarating to watch.

Some of the riders were throwing themselves under their horses' bellies and firing at full gallop.

The yelling and shouting must, she thought, be some kind of war cry.

She felt the Bedouins would ride right into them and there would be a dreadful collision, but at the last second they pulled their horses back onto their haunches.

It was a brilliant display of horsemanship.

In fact now it was over it seemed almost impossible that it had ever happened.

The Earl and Charles were congratulating the Sheik.

"Your men are wonderful," they both said.

Now they were standing by the panting horses and led by the Sheik, Vanda was taken from horse to horse.

The Sheik introduced her and she was quite certain he made her sound very impressive. The riders bowed to her and she managed to say in Arabic to each one that he was a very good rider.

When the tribesmen dispersed, the Sheik said they should go home.

"The next time we come," he said, "we will stay here. Perhaps in three or four day's time."

Vanda looked quickly at the Earl

"I am afraid, Your Highness," he said, "we will have left you by then."

"Oh, but that would be a mistake," the Sheik protested. "I have many more animals to show you and horses from further towards the Euphrates are being brought here for your inspection."

"I still think, Your Highness, it will be impossible for us to stay longer than perhaps three more days. You will understand that I have many responsibilities in England and I cannot be away too long."

The Sheik did not protest further, but there was an expression on his face which made Vanda believe he was determined to keep them.

When they returned to the house it was getting late and nearly time for dinner.

Vanda was now feeling a little tired and was glad to rest and she hoped that they would not stay up too late. They had certainly not been so last night, but she suspected that the Sheik had planned another entertainment for this evening.

Heading towards her bedroom, she walked first into the sitting room where she had eaten breakfast and Charles followed her where they were alone.

For the moment there was no sign of the two Bedouin Ladies-in-Waiting.

"Favin and I," Charles told her in a low voice, "have chosen at least twenty horses we would like to buy, but our host is being rather difficult about it. I wonder if there is any chance of you persuading him."

"I will do my best, but I certainly thought he had promised you that if you brought him a Royal Princess, he would allow you to buy a number of his horses."

"I think he intends to give us perhaps three or four as a present," Charles replied. "But we want more than that."

"I do not blame you. They are the most beautiful creatures I have ever seen."

"I think the same, so do please see what you can do for us at dinner."

Vanda chose one of her prettiest gowns and decided to wear the best pieces of the jewellery the Earl had lent her.

She had almost forgotten about the Earl's jewel case. Her maid at Brackenshaw House had told her that she had put it into the suitcase which contained her hair brushes.

She opened the jewel case and found that it contained the most spectacular and beautiful necklace she had ever seen.

There was a huge diamond in the pendant which hung from the centre of the necklace and it was matched by the same design on a bracelet.

She felt as she entered the room where they would dine that the Sheik should certainly be impressed, although the Earl and her brother might think she was slightly overdressed.

She did in fact notice a twinkle in the Earl's eye as she crossed the room.

All three men bowed gracefully to her.

They waited until she had seated herself on the same sofa as last night. She was next to the Sheik again and turning to him she said,

"I cannot tell you, Your Highness, how much I have enjoyed today. It a day I shall always remember."

"I am so glad that Your Royal Highness is pleased." the Sheik answered. "Our men were all very honoured to perform in front of you, and I am glad there were no casualties as they can sometimes occur when they become overexcited."

"I could not bear to think of any casualties to your

marvellous horses," Vanda remarked. "I am only hoping that I shall not have to say goodbye to too many of them when I return home."

She paused for a moment before she added beguilingly,

"I want to remember that this was the happiest time of my life whenever I see an Arab horse."

The Sheik smiled.

"That is what I hope you will always do and my present which I shall give to you will be a white stallion just for you."

Vanda clasped her hands together.

"Your Highness is too kind. How can I thank you for such a marvellous gift?"

The Sheik did not answer and after a moment she said,

"You know that the Earl and his friend are planning to run your horses in every race they can enter in England. Your Highness must come and see them run and feel rewarded when they run faster than any other horse in the races."

"I do not think I could do that," the Sheik replied wistfully.

"But of course you can," Vanda encouraged him. "If we have enough horses to take back, then it will be possible to enter them in all the great Classic races of England."

The Sheik gave her a sharp glance.

She guessed he was fully conscious of where she was leading him.

"I will think about it," he murmured after a pause.

At that moment the servants came in with dinner and Vanda had been right in forecasting that there would be another performance.

The meal was very much the same as they had eaten

the night before and when it was finished the curtains at the end of the room were drawn back.

This time a magician appeared who conjured up strange creatures including snakes which danced when he played to them and birds which apparently came from nowhere fluttered overhead.

It was a very skilful performance and Vanda was entranced by the magician. He was followed by the same dancers as last night performing more ordinary Eastern dancing and they looked no less attractive as they did so.

Finally one dancer came on who was obviously intended to be the star of the evening and as soon as she began to dance the Earl glanced at Charles as they both knew what they were about to see.

There were dancers in the East who were known for their sensuous performances and although men found it enjoyable it was unsuitable in every way for Vanda.

The Earl was strongly of the opinion that he would dislike Vanda in her innocence to witness anything so exotic and that certainly included the dance they were about to see.

He was sitting next to Vanda.

Unexpectedly he bent towards her and taking her hand pressed it firmly.

"I can see Your Royal Highness is feeling a little faint," he said. "It is not surprising after the heat of the day. Let me assist you to your bedroom."

He spoke loud enough for the Sheik to hear.

Vanda, after one surprised look, realised from the pressure of his hand what she must do. She half shut her eyes and the Earl put his arm round her and lifted her to her feet.

Then, as she seemed particularly limp, he carried her from the room.

It all happened before the Sheik could make any movement or ask what was happening.

Outside the Earl carried Vanda down the passages towards her room. Only when there was no one to hear them did he say,

"Please understand that what you were about to see was not suitable for your eyes."

"Why not?" Vanda questioned.

The Earl could think of many answers but he replied,

"The dance is somewhat improper and after it has taken place the Sheik will doubtless be shocked at his own foolishness in allowing the performance."

"Then I am glad you were clever enough to warn me," Vanda said. "Although I am rather sorry not to see the dance."

"It is something you would not enjoy nor understand," the Earl counselled almost sharply. "And thank you for what you said to the Sheik. I am hoping it will make him part with more horses than he intends to do at the moment."

He had no wish to go on talking about the dance.

Vanda however understood what he was doing, but she wondered why it would matter so much what she might witness. She could not imagine the dancer could do anything that was really shocking.

She did however remember that her father had talked about the Eastern dancers. He had seen some performances in various places where her mother had never accompanied him.

The Earl took her to her room and laid her gently on her bed.

"Quite frankly," Vanda sighed, "although I may be missing something exciting, I am quite happy to go to bed. We have done such a lot today."

"You have been absolutely splendid," the Earl said.

There was only one lamp burning in her bedroom but the Earl thought as it shone on her face how glorious she looked, and it struck him that if he had carried any other woman as he had just carried Vanda, she would expect him to kiss her.

It was something he would be very willing to do.

Vanda however moved towards her dressing table and said,

"As there is no sign of my Ladies-in-Waiting would you be very kind and undo the beautiful necklace you lent me? I am afraid of damaging it and it has such a difficult clasp."

The Earl smiled as he walked up behind her.

She had sat down on the sofa in front of her dressing table.

He had to bend very close in order to see the fastening clearly. It was cleverly made and hidden behind the design of the necklace itself and it took him some time to find how it unfastened.

He became conscious as he did so of the soft whiteness of Vanda's skin and that her evening gown was cut particularly low at the back.

Vanda pulled the necklace forward once it was undone.

The Earl wondered what she would do if he bent and kissed the back of her neck. He had kissed so many women in this way when he was removing their jewellery.

Vanda bent forward to place the necklace back into its velvet case. As she did so she said,

"It was so kind of you to lend me something so beautiful. I am only terrified in case it is stolen from me or I lose it."

95

The Earl walked towards the door.

"Goodnight, Vanda," he called. "It has been a most eventful day and perhaps we shall have an even better one tomorrow. Sleep well."

He walked out as he finished speaking and Vanda heard his footsteps going down the passage. She wished he had stayed a little longer and talked some more to her.

They had not had a chance to be alone ever since they had left the yacht.

Vanda thought now that he must be in a hurry to return to the performance to see the exotic dancer and she wondered if he would find her very exciting.

Certainly more amusing than she herself could be.

'He is very handsome,' she thought, 'and no one could be kinder or more considerate than he has been to Charles and me.'

She sat at her dressing table thinking of the Earl when the two Bedouin women came hurrying into the room full of apologies.

They had thought she would not go to bed until the entertainment was over.

"More dancing is yet to come," they said. "But we understand Your Royal Highness is tired."

"It has been a very long day," Vanda replied, feeling that she need not make any further explanations.

Until she finally fell asleep she remembered once again how the Earl had carried her, as if she weighed nothing, down the corridor and into her bedroom.

*

The next morning Charles came to her room while she was having her breakfast.

The two Bedouin women who were sitting on the floor rose when he appeared.

After bowing perfunctorily, he said,

"I would request a private word with Your Royal Highness."

The two women understood and disappeared.

When they had gone, Vanda looked at her brother.

"What is the matter? I know by the expression on your face that you are troubled."

"It is something which happened last night after you had left," Charles replied.

He pulled a sofa near to her and sat down so that he did not have to raise his voice.

"Is something wrong?" Vanda asked.

"I am afraid it is something which will upset you."

Vanda looked at him more critically.

"It has obviously upset *you*. What is it? Tell me!"

"You are not going to like this, Vanda," Charles began. "But for the moment Favin and I are at a loss as to how to resolve the problem."

"What is it?" Vanda asked again, becoming agitated.

"After you had gone to bed and the show was over, which I may say was most unsuitable for you, we started to talk to the Sheik again about his horses."

"Did he say you could buy any more?" Vanda asked eagerly.

Charles paused a moment.

"He actually said that we can have as many as we like but on one condition."

"What was that?" Vanda questioned.

"You are not going to like this and it is very uncomfortable for all of us," Charles answered. "But he said that if you stayed, we could take any horses we wanted."

Vanda looked at her brother in sheer astonishment.

"What do you mean," she demanded, "if I stayed?"

"I think the Sheik wants to marry you, or at any rate to keep you with him to impress the other tribes as he is impressing them now by having you here."

"Of course I cannot – do – that," Vanda stammered. "How did you answer him?"

"We said it was impossible and Favin was in fact very astute with the Sheik."

"In – what – way?" Vanda asked nervously.

"He said he was quite certain that Queen Victoria would not allow you to stay even if you wanted to, and we had promised Her Majesty that we would bring you back safely."

"And what did the Sheik say to that?"

"He was not particularly affected. In fact he seemed to think that, if you stayed here and ruled with him over his tribe and his horses, you would enjoy it more than being just one of the many Princesses there are in England."

Vanda thought that the Earl's argument was rather clever, but at the same time she was becoming frightened.

"Did you make it – absolutely – clear that I cannot – stay?"

"We both insisted that it was impossible, but you know what Sheiks are like. They think they are a sort of God in their own particular territory. He was in fact offering you half of his Kingdom."

Vanda made a helpless gesture with her hands.

"What are we – going to – do?"

"Leave as soon as we can," Charles answered. "And be content with as many horses as he condescends to allow us to take."

"That is not enough," Vanda cried. "Oh, Charles, what can I do to persuade him to let us have more?"

"Favin thinks you must do nothing," Charles said quickly. "We sat up late talking about it and he is determined you should not be involved in what has become a very difficult situation."

His voice sharpened as he continued,

"If the Sheik says anything, you are to pretend you do not understand. We must try to wangle out of him a few more horses than he has already promised and then go home."

Vanda gave a deep sigh.

She knew how much this meant both to the Earl and Charles. They would have *some* horses, yet after what they had seen yesterday they obviously wanted a great many more.

"I – am – so sorry," she whispered beneath her breath.

"It's not your fault," Charles protested. "You have done your best – in fact done it too well. He is like a greedy little boy who, having been given one piece of cake, wants the rest of it all for himself."

Vanda chuckled.

"I don't think calling me a cake is much of a compliment, but I understand what you mean."

"What you have to do is to be charming at the festival, or whatever he calls it, this afternoon. Then we will try to leave tomorrow or the next day."

Vanda gave an anguished cry,

"I was so hoping you would make lots of money from the horses when we return to England."

"That is what I was hoping too, but we will have to be content with what he gives us and I am sure it is no use arguing with a Sheik."

Vanda bent forward and kissed her brother.

"I hate you to be disappointed," she sighed. "We had

hoped for so much from this trip and of course it has cost the Earl so much."

"He can afford it," Charles said, "but we cannot. It is no use pretending, Vanda, we need a great deal more money than we have at the moment to keep our stables going and to have something decent to sell."

Vanda knew he was thinking of the horses he could not acquire.

She kissed him again.

"Cheer up, Charles, perhaps at the last moment just as we are stepping on the *Sea Serpent* a man will come out of the crowd and offer you ten magnificent stallions."

"If he could throw in ten good mares," Chares said, "I would be walking straight into Heaven. But as it is I must be content with small mercies."

He rose and would have walked towards the door if Vanda had not stopped him.

"You are quite certain the Sheik will not try to keep me here anyway?" she asked tremulously.

"He is too sensible to think he could kidnap you and anyway it is something which we must not allow to happen, because to get you back we should have to explain to the British Embassy that you are not Her Royal Highness but just unimportant Miss Kenwood."

"Now you are being unkind and making me feel small and unwanted."

"You could never be that, but enjoy yourself as Royalty, because after tomorrow you will just be yourself and my sister, who is very pretty if nothing else!"

Vanda picked up a cushion and threw it at him.

"Go away, I am very sorry all this has happened. At the same time I intend to enjoy myself this afternoon. Not because of the people who have come to stare at me, but because I want to drink in all those marvellous horses for the last time so that I will never forget them."

"Nor could I," Charles said as he reached the door. "Equally I would rather take them with me than leave them in the desert!"

Vanda thought he always had the last word.

The Bedouin women came back and she started to dress.

She began to pray with all her heart that the Sheik would relent and Charles and the Earl would obtain the number of horses they desired.

'The Sheik has so many,' she mused, 'he will hardly miss a dozen or so. Perhaps by a miracle I may be able to persuade him to be generous.'

She tried to think how she could succeed, but there was obviously no easy way.

She could only go on praying and hoping that someone in Heaven was hearing her prayer.

CHAPTER SIX

Vanda was awoken early by the sound of the camp rising. She listened to the chatter of voices, the bleating of the goats and the lambs being moved out to pasture.

There was laughter from the children and yells of delight as they found something new to play with.

After a while she rose and dressed.

The Bedouin women came to help her into the most dazzling dress she had brought with her.

It was in the stunning pink of the sky when the sun is about to rise and was trimmed as only a French designer can trim a gown to make it outstanding. With it she wore an extremely pretty hat with roses of the same colour.

After she had breakfasted alone, she felt as she went to find the others that the Sheik would undoubtedly be impressed by her appearance.

The gentlemen were waiting for her and she realised that they all were dressed in their best.

Sheik Abu was magnificently dressed in white with a flashing ornament in his turban and in his belt there were knives with jewelled handles and also, she thought, a revolver.

While Vanda had been dressing she had heard the sound of the arrivals and like all Bedouins the more noise they made the more important they appeared.

As soon as they moved out of the house she could see groups of horses assembling. The tribesmen wore variously coloured *abbas*. She recognised that these marked the different tribes which were friendly to Sheik Abu.

She knew that the Sheik of one other tribe was an enemy and she had asked the Earl when she found the opportunity what was the name of that Sheik.

"Sheik Shalaan el Hassein," he answered. "He is also the enemy of Sheik Abdul Medjvel el Mezrab."

Vanda remembered that the latter was the name of the Sheik who had married the beautiful Lady Jane Digby.

"Is he coming today?" she asked eagerly as it would be so fascinating to meet him after there had been so much talk about him and the English woman he had married.

"I think he lives too far away," the Earl replied, "but there are quite enough tribes here who consider themselves of even greater stature."

They certainly put on a very good performance. Again and again the different tribes galloped up to where the Sheik and Vanda were sitting in the reviewing stand.

They were waving their lances and performing feats even more daring than the Sheik's tribe had attempted. Vanda was frightened in case they should fall to the ground or worse still, injure their horses.

When all the newcomers had made their obeisance to the Sheik, the tribes arranged themselves in order in front of them.

This was so that Vanda could meet them as the Sheik had told them that she wished to do.

She walked to inspect the horses and following her were the Earl and Charles who were as eager as she was and as she looked at the horses, they told her which were the best.

As she did so she realised that the Earl had been right

when he said how tame and affectionate the Arab horses could be. The mares nuzzled against Vanda as she patted them.

The Sheik in charge of each tribe had literally to push the horses to one side to show her the ones he particularly wanted her to notice.

There was one stallion which totally thrilled her. It belonged to a young Sheik who had only recently taken over the leadership of his tribe from his father.

He looked at Vanda with admiring eyes and announced,

"This, Your Royal Highness, is a *Kehilan*."

The stallion was indeed magnificent and the young Sheik continued,

"The breed received its name from the black marks round their eyes. The marks give them the appearance of being painted with kohl like the Arab women."

He paused before he added in a low voice,

"But they are not as beautiful as Your Royal Highness!"

Vanda smiled at him.

"Thank you," she blushed. "But I find everything in your country so beautiful, especially the horses."

As if he was annoyed at the young Sheik for trying to flirt with her, the Sheik moved Vanda way.

He told her, as if he was giving her a lecture, that the Bedouins never use a bit or bridle of any sort for their horses – only a halter with a fine chain fastened round the nose.

"I noticed your men riding like that," Vanda said, "and I find it extraordinary that they can control their horses so easily and so efficiently."

"I think it is because our animals are gentle and without vices," the Sheik replied. "They have none of the viciousness of European animals."

"How does it happen that there are such especially fine breeds in Syria?" Vanda asked.

"There is a legend which says they are descended from the mares of King Solomon, but few Arabs believe it. What we do know is that our horses have a strain which is incomparable with any other in the world."

The Sheik spoke almost aggressively, as if he expected her to contradict him.

Vanda responded quietly,

"We in England agree entirely."

She paused before adding a little tentatively,

"That is why we are so anxious to buy a good number of horses from you, Your Highness."

The Sheik did not answer and she felt her spirits fall.

It would be tragic if they returned to England with only three horses when they needed so many more, but she understood however that it would be a mistake to go on bothering the Sheik.

She was glad when a little while later there was a tolling of bells from the house to signal that luncheon was ready.

The Sheik had certainly done his guests proud. The large room in which they had dined earlier had been flung open with all the curtains drawn back.

There were low tables all round the room and the display in the centre of fruit and flowers was very beautiful.

The food was placed on the tables so it was easy for everyone to help themselves whilst the servants hovered around offering the soft fruit drinks which were all the Bedouins ever drank.

There was no wine this time for the Earl and Charles, which made Vanda realise how privileged they had been to be allowed wine when they were alone with the Sheik the previous evening.

She was again seated on his right.

On the other side of her was the young Sheik who had paid her the compliment and she was not surprised to learn that he was the head of the largest tribe present.

She noticed that the other guests were very respectful towards him and she therefore addressed him as Your Highness, knowing that he was pleased that she acknowledged him as an eminent Sheik.

Vanda enjoyed the *kemmáye* which seemed even more appetising than on the previous day and there was a profusion of quail's eggs and magnificent bowls of fruit.

She noticed that all the guests ate eagerly.

By the time they were finished the tables which had been so laden seemed almost empty.

The Earl whispered to Vanda that she would now be expected to ride. She was delighted at the idea and hurried to her bedroom followed by her Bedouin ladies.

She quickly changed into her pink riding habit, convinced that it was the more spectacular of the two she had bought in London. There was a gauze veil of the same colour around her black hat.

She wanted to make her appearance even more impressive and therefore took a diamond brooch from the Earl's jewellery box and pinned it onto her left shoulder.

She looked at herself in the mirror and thought the Sheik would definitely be proud to show her off to his friends.

She walked outside to discover that they were already waiting for her and so were the horses.

She was to be mounted on a magnificent white mare which she thought the Sheik had deliberately chosen for her because she would look spectacular on it. Her ears were long and her eyes were full and soft.

"She is very lovely!" Vanda exclaimed.

"She is a *Hamdani*," the Sheik informed her. "A very uncommon breed both amongst the Aeneze and our own tribe."

"Allow me to assist Your Royal Highness," a voice came from behind Vanda.

She turned her head to see the young Sheik who had sat next to her at luncheon. Before she could say anything he had lifted her up and placed her on the saddle.

She became aware as he did so that her host was looking extremely indignant.

"Thank you so much," Vanda said to the young Sheik.

"You can come and visit me," he invited her, "and I will show you two horses of the same breed, one of which I assure you is even more magnificent than this one."

"I find that hard to believe."

While she was talking her host had mounted his horse and now he said almost angrily to Vanda,

"Come, Your Royal Highness. We have a great deal to do."

He rode away without speaking to the young Sheik, who hurried to his own horse so that he could follow them.

The Sheik took Vanda round the horses of each tribe whose Chief had been a guest at luncheon. She had already been introduced to all of them, yet she realised that they in their turn wanted to impress their tribes by showing how friendly they were with the Royal Princess.

Most of the men could not understand English so all Vanda's comments were translated by the Sheik and because her words were always of praise she was deeply appreciated.

It took them quite a long time to go round all the different tribes.

Vanda was in no doubt that additional tribes had arrived while they were having luncheon.

They were some distance away from the house when there was the sound of a gunshot followed by several others.

The Sheik turned his horse round to look back and there appeared to be some commotion in front of his house.

From the distance Vanda could not see what was happening.

A number of tribesmen started to ride towards the turmoil and there must have been a dozen or more men in front of her riding towards the house.

She was suddenly aware that two horses had closed in beside hers.

She looked at them.

They were ridden by men who seemed at first glance to be differently dressed from any of the tribesmen she had seen so far.

She was just about to speak to them hoping they would understand her, when to her astonishment they seized the reins of her mare and without a word they started to lead her swiftly away into the desert.

"What are you doing? What is happening?" Vanda demanded.

Even as she spoke the two men on either side of her quickened their horses and started to gallop, pulling her horse with them.

"Stop! Who are you? Where are you going?"

She quickly began to realise that she was being kidnapped and she could only imagine it was by the enemy of Sheik Abu. She remembered that the Earl had told her his name was Sheik Shalaan el Hassein.

It took Vanda a moment or two to appreciate the horror of her situation and it was equally difficult to think.

The two men were setting such a tremendous pace that she had to be careful not to fall off and their horses were perfectly willing to go faster and faster.

She had never galloped faster than she was now being forced to do by the two men on either side of her.

When she managed to glance at them she felt that they were men of perhaps thirty years of age and she guessed from the way they were dressed that they were of some importance.

She wondered what the Sheik would do when he found that she was missing.

There were obviously tribesmen near them when she had been kidnapped who would recognise the men who had taken her.

It was a gross insult to have snatched away the Sheik's Royal guest and it would undoubtedly mean war between the tribes.

The whole idea was terrifying.

Vanda could not bear to think that many horses would be wounded or killed, but she was frightened for herself. Somehow, she believed, the Earl would get her back, but at what cost?

It was still difficult to think clearly because of the pace at which they were still galloping.

Then, sooner than she expected she saw ahead a cluster of black tents and sensed that this must be where the tribe was camped.

It was only when they were a short distance away that the two men on each side of her slowed down a little.

As they drew nearer Vanda could see a crowd of tribesmen congregating, some on horseback, some standing, but they were all looking in her direction.

What had just happened, she thought, must have been skilfully planned, as the horsemen came rushing towards her, waving and shouting with excitement.

She could imagine the plot without being told.

Sheik Shalaan el Hassein had wished deliberately to insult his enemy and he could not have done so more effectively than by abducting his chief guest who was believed to be a Royal Princess.

When the men on horseback reached her they just stared at her and turned their horses to ride on beside them.

Now Vanda's two captors had slowed down to a trot as the crowd outside the tents were moving towards her. They were obviously roused by her appearance and by the fact that she was a prisoner.

With difficulty she straightened her shoulders, lifted her head and looked over towards the tents.

From the largest tent a man emerged dressed in full flowing robes looking most imposing and very much in charge.

Her two captors drew her right up to him and the Sheik looked directly over the horse's head at Vanda.

In quite good English he announced,

"Your Royal Highness, Princess Vanda, I am Sheik Shalaan el Hussein and you are my prisoner!"

Vanda inclined her head.

"I guessed, Your Highness," she stated in a cold voice, "what was happening to me, but this is an outrage."

There was a faint smile on the Sheik Shalaan's face as he replied,

"I was not invited to the party and I had therefore to ask the chief guest to come to me!"

From the way he spoke Vanda realised he was as well educated as Sheik Abu.

The two men who had kidnapped her dismounted and then to her surprise Sheik Shalaan lifted her to the ground.

"I think," he said, "Your Royal Highness would like to partake of some refreshment after such an unexpected ride."

Vanda did not answer, she only allowed him to lead her into his tent, which was similar to the one they had taken luncheon in yesterday.

The same low tables, carpets, sofas and curtains which shut out the sun.

Sheik Shalaan moved a sofa towards the table and with a sense of relief, because she was so frightened, Vanda sat down.

At least, she thought, she was being treated in a civilised manner and with respect.

As soon as she was seated, a drink of fruit juice was set in front of her. She took a sip before she became aware that Sheik Shalaan had not sat down but was standing looking at her.

He did not speak and after a moment Vanda quizzed him,

"Now, having kidnapped me, what do you intend to do with me?"

"I am waiting to see what the reaction of the enemy will be," the Sheik replied. "Whatever it is you can be sure my men will be ready for them and I shall not give up such a beautiful Princess easily."

Vanda put down her glass.

"Please," she pleaded, "settle this dispute amicably. If you fight the horses will be hurt and perhaps many of your men will be killed. Is it worth losing such valuable assets for anyone, even an English Princess?"

The Sheik gave a surprised laugh.

"You are very brave," he said, "as I have been told the English are. At the same time I have managed to hurt my enemy in a manner he will not forget."

He paused before continuing,

"He was flaunting Your Royal Highness before his friends and his enemies to show how important and how prestigious he is. Now he will be a laughing stock. The man who lost his prize even while it was still within his grasp."

There was a jeering note in the Sheik's voice. It told Vanda how delighted he was to hurt Sheik Abu Hamid.

For a moment she wondered what she could say and then because she realised how pleased the Sheik was with himself, she said,

"I think in fact, Your Highness, you are being both unkind and childish. Is what you have just done worth the life of even one of your magnificent horses or perhaps a number of your faithful followers?"

The Sheik made an expressive gesture with his hands.

"What else can you expect from us living in the desert?" he asked. "But to fight and demonstrate our superiority and strength."

"I can imagine other actions which would be far more civilised," Vanda responded.

As she spoke she noticed a look in the Sheik's eyes which frightened her.

He was, she thought, not as old as she had expected him to be. Perhaps approaching forty, but no older.

For the first time since she had arrived in the Sheik's tent she was frightened for herself as a woman. Suppose he avenged himself on Sheik Abu by assaulting her? Or perhaps, without even thinking of his revenge, he would find her desirable.

Quickly, because it was the first idea that came into her head, she said,

"I only hope, Your Highness, that before you take any action you will give not only Sheik Abu, but the two distinguished Englishmen who have accompanied me here to your country, a chance to solve this problem. Perhaps they can find a solution which will be to your advantage without bloodshed."

"I think it is quite unnecessary," the Sheik Shalaan retorted, "for Englishmen to take any part in what is a conflict between Sheik Abu and me."

"As I am English, then obviously the English must be concerned. I can sure you, Your Highness, that if I am hurt, upset or insulted, the stern attention of Her Majesty Queen Victoria will be invoked."

She realised as she spoke that this thought had never occurred to the Sheik. In truth it did perturb him as the might and importance of the British Empire was indisputable.

Vanda was quite certain that the fact of her being English would involve the British Empire had never crossed the Sheik Shalaan's mind.

"I can only ask," she continued, "that Your Highness will think over carefully what I have said. As I have already suggested, please wait for developments before you take any hasty steps in one direction or another."

She rose to her feet as she finished speaking saying,

"I think, since I find my treatment very disturbing, I would like to lie down."

The Sheik clapped his hands and when a servant appeared he gave him some hurried orders.

The Sheik and Vanda sat in heavy silence.

A few minutes late two women hurried into the room.

"These women will take you to a tent where I hope

you will be comfortable. A little later I shall be most disappointed if Your Royal Highness will not dine with me. Until then, pray rest."

Vanda acknowledged his words with a little nod of her head and then seeing where the women had moved to on the other side of the room, she joined them.

She did not look back, but she sensed that the Sheik was watching her keenly.

She was troubled by the expression in his eyes.

The tent to which she was taken was a grand one and she thought it was doubtless the most important tent next to the Sheik's own. It was not one that would usually be allotted to a prisoner.

Because she was hot and tired she took off her hat, her riding jacket and her boots and lay on top of the bed which was more like a couch.

The soft pillows were a relief as ever since the horsemen had come on each side of her she had been tense with anxiety.

Now she could only hope that Sheik Shalaan would negotiate. Perhaps he would send a message which the Earl and Sheik Abu could discuss together.

It was indeed a dramatic and perhaps a tragic ending to their adventure, although Vanda felt strongly that she would do anything rather than allow the two tribes to fight over her.

The horses were all so beautiful and she could not bear to think of them wounded and dying.

She knew that desert wars were just a way of proving each Sheik's superiority.

She must have dozed for a while.

When the women came to wake her she found that it was already late and it must in fact be getting on for eight o'clock.

Darkness had arrived with its usual swiftness and when she walked into the centre of the tent the lights were lit.

Sheik Shalaan was waiting for her and when they were seated with a low table in front of them Vanda asked,

"Have you heard anything from Sheik Abu?"

"Nothing, Your Royal Highness," he replied sharply.

This omission had obviously surprised him and Vanda guessed that he was worried at the silence.

"If we cannot discuss the current situation," Vanda said, "perhaps you tell me about your tribe? I am also interested to know why you are an enemy of Sheik Abdul Medjvel el Mezrab."

Sheik Shalaan turned to her in surprise.

"How do you know that?" he asked.

Vanda smiled.

"His wife is English and of course in England we have all been most interested in her very colourful and unusual career."

The Sheik laughed.

"Unusual is the right word for it, Your Royal Highness. And I find it extraordinary that an English woman should wish to be a Bedouin's wife."

He paused before he enquired,

"Would you?"

Vanda shook her head.

"I would love his horses and enjoy some aspects of life in the desert, but when I marry I would wish it to be to an Englishman."

She spoke very positively and the Sheik asked her,

"You would not for instance think of enjoying a life here with me?"

Vanda shook her head again.

"We live in different worlds. If you desire happiness I think you should find it in your own world in which there are many beautiful women. They would love you as you wish to be loved, not as a Sheik but as a man."

The Sheik seemed to have difficulty finding his words before answering.

Then he said,

"My women love me because they admire me."

Vanda shook her head.

"If they admire you as a Sheik, that is not love. What every woman wants and every man for that matter, is someone who loves them for themselves regardless of whether they are a King or a pauper, a Sheik or a slave."

"Do you think it possible I could find such a woman?"

"If you have not found her already, there is still every possibility," Vanda replied. "I have always been told that to the Arabs the stars are very important and some of them believe, like the gypsies, that there is a star for every man and woman. What you should be looking for is the woman who belongs to your star, and when you find her you will know real love and real happiness."

Sheik Shalaan looked at her again in surprise.

"I never thought of it in such a way," he admitted. "But I suppose you are saying that is what the beautiful Lady Jane found with her Sheik."

"Of course. She had several other husbands, but none of them was the right man. She knew he was somewhere in the world and she found him in the desert."

As she finished speaking she thought that perhaps this Sheik had also been in love with the beautiful Jane Digby and maybe that was why he was the enemy of her husband besides being the enemy of Sheik Abu Hamid.

She realised she had given him something to think about.

She added as if to make it easier for him,

"I think you should look amongst the women of your own country first. It would be easier for both of you than if you have to grow accustomed to strange habits, different standards and, of course most important of all, different religions."

"I understand what you are saying to me. On the other hand there are many, many women in the world and I find it difficult to believe that one will be so very different for me from all the others."

"She will be when you find her," Vanda assured him. "Then you will realise that you have found the other part of yourself and you will be happy until you both die."

She spoke so positively that Sheik Shalaan stared at her as if she was a Prophet or even a clairvoyant looking into his future.

To keep him interested Vanda continued talking about the happiness her father and mother had found together, and men and women throughout history who had searched the world until they found their true love and for whom their quest was like the Golden Fleece or the Holy Grail.

It was quite late when, almost like a child who had been listening to a fairy tale, the Sheik agreed that it was time to retire.

"Tomorrow morning," Vanda suggested, "I am sure there will be a message, and then perhaps, Your Highness, we can discuss together the best way to respond."

"I can only thank you," the Sheik said, "for a very interesting and a most unusual evening. I have never before, Your Royal Highness, talked to a woman as I have talked to you tonight."

Vanda stretched out her hand and he raised it to his lips.

"Sleep well," he said. "You will not be disturbed."

She understood as he spoke that he was reassuring her and the relief was almost like a stone being lifted from her breast.

She had been afraid, of course she had been afraid.

Perhaps, she thought, he might assault her in his desire to avenge himself on Sheik Abu.

As she walked away from him towards her tent, she felt certain that at any rate she was safe for tonight.

She still thought it strange that there had been no message from Sheik Abu or the Earl and her brother.

She was very conscious that Sheik Shalaan was waiting for them to attack and when she looked out from her tent, she could see that his men were armed and ready, their horses beside them.

If their enemy appeared they could go into battle in a few seconds.

Vanda was helped out of her clothes by the two Bedouin women. For dinner she had only been able to remove her riding jacket and now she took off her skirt and her pretty white chiffon blouse.

There was no sign of any sort of nightgown so she thought the only thing she could do was to sleep in the lace-trimmed vest she wore, and she would keep on the petticoat which went under her riding skirt.

She informed the two Bedouin women what she would do by gesturing with her hands.

Then she climbed into bed.

They were surprised but understood and bowing low they eventually went away and left her alone.

Vanda lay back against the soft cushions and it was too warm for the moment for her to need any covers over her.

She closed her eyes and started to pray that there would be no bloodshed between the tribes.

Apart from anything else, it would be dangerous if news of a tribal battle was broadcast too widely. The British Embassies in Beirut or Damascus might communicate with London and it would soon be discovered there was no one known to the Royal family as Princess Vanda of Thessaly.

'Please God – help us – *please*,' Vanda prayed.

She believed that her prayer was going straight to Heaven and the stars which were shining brightly outside would carry it up into the sky.

'Perhaps – the Earl will rescue – me,' she wondered.

Then she prayed that he would be brave enough to do so.

*

When it was discovered, and it took a little time, that Vanda was missing, there was much consternation.

Some of the less important Sheiks had hurried to the house to tell Sheik Abu that they had seen the Royal Princess being abducted.

The two riders, they conjectured, belonged to the Hassein tribe.

At first Sheik Abu did not believe the story.

"How is it possible?" he kept asking. "How could it have happened with all my men around?"

His immediate impulse was to lead all the tribes to attack Sheik Shalaan and kill every man of his tribe.

The Earl immediately appreciated the danger of such a course of action and quickly, because the Sheik was in such a towering rage, he cautioned,

"Be careful – very careful."

"Why should I be careful?" Sheik Abu stormed. "Once and for all I will exterminate that despicable man and all his tribe."

"Before you attempt any such attack," the Earl advised, "you must understand that you will have the whole of Beirut and Damascus laughing at you. Sheik Shalaan spirited away your Royal guest in the middle of your party. They will not commiserate with Your Highness, but snigger at you."

Sheik Abu quietened and there was absolute silence before he asked,

"What then can I do?"

"I think with a little luck I might bring her back," the Earl answered slowly.

The Sheik gazed at him in astonishment.

"How could you possibly do it?"

"I have an idea. I may be wrong, but I think it is an off-chance that is worth trying."

"Anything is worth trying if we can find Vanda," Charles added sharply.

"I know," the Earl replied, "but we do not need a scandal and at all costs we must avoid bloodshed."

He did not have to explain to Charles what he meant by a scandal.

The two men looked at each other and the Earl knew that Charles understood.

"Then what can you do?" Sheik Abu demanded. "I cannot permit that devil to take away my honoured guest without striking at him with every weapon at my command."

"If it is at all possible and with the help of Allah," the Earl declared, "we will arrange it so that Her Royal Highness is safe and you do not need to lose face."

"I will give you thirty of my best Arab horses if you are successful, but personally I think it is impossible."

"Let me try it my way," the Earl demanded, "and if I

fail, then we will assist you with *your* solution. That is my bargain."

He held out his hand as he spoke and the Sheik felt obliged to take it, but he was extremely dubious as to whether the Earl could achieve anything and because he was sure that in the end his men would be required to free the Princess.

He promptly left the Earl and Charles to go and see how much ammunition there was in store and to check that every man in his tribe was well armed.

It was growing late in the afternoon and a number of the neighbouring tribesmen had moved away without realising what had happened.

The Sheik did not bid farewell to those of his guests who had not yet departed as at the moment he was still tense with anger.

His greatest enemy had stolen a march on him when he least expected it and yet he realised that the Earl was speaking the truth.

If what had happened became known all over Syria, he would undoubtedly become a laughing stock.

'I have to do something drastic,' he said to himself.

However he felt restrained for the moment by the quiet and confident way the Earl was behaving.

Inside the tent Charles asked,

"What the *hell* are you going to do, Favin?"

I have an idea or perhaps it is a premonition, but I don't want to talk about it. I can only hope and pray that I will be successful."

"As you can imagine I am praying too," Charles assured him. "Vanda must be terrified by what is happening to her."

He paused for a moment before he asked,

"You do not think, you do not imagine, Favin, they will hurt her in any way? You know these damn people better than I do."

"I think they will respect her," the Earl responded quietly, "because she is British and because they believe her to be Royal."

"I can only hope you are right. If not, I think I will go out and kill somebody."

The Earl did not answer. He merely walked out of the tent to find Carstairs. He needed something very important which he knew only Carstairs could find for him.

Then in his own room he went to the window and looked up at the sky. He had sounded very confident talking to Charles that Vanda would not be abused. However within himself he was suddenly very afraid for her.

She was so young, so innocent.

As he knew only too well, she had no knowledge of men. How could she cope with a man, especially a Bedouin, who desired her?

He could imagine her fear, her terror and her humiliation.

The very idea seemed to stab him as if by a dagger.

It was then that he admitted to himself something he had known for a long time – that he loved her.

CHAPTER SEVEN

Vanda was dreaming of the Earl.

She thought he was kissing her.

Then suddenly she awoke to find that he was!

His lips were on hers and a strange feeling she had never known seemed to whirl through her body and senses.

Thinking it could not be true, she opened her eyes and in the faint light filtering into the tent she could see the Earl kneeling beside her.

She would have spoken but once against his lips were on hers. She understood that he was telling her to keep quiet and when he raised his head he placed his finger on her lips.

She wanted him to kiss her and go on kissing her and nothing else mattered in the whole world.

The Earl rose slowly to his feet and began to pull Vanda from the bed.

Following him she tip-toed across the floor trying to think of how he could have entered the tent and then at the very back she could see a faint chink of moonlight.

A moment later the Earl bent down to the ground and started to squeeze himself through what Vanda now realised was a cutting at the bottom of the tent.

He moved very slowly and she thought he was almost like a snake slithering across the floor.

Once he was outside he reached out for her hand and pulled her forward. She managed to squeeze through the opening in the same way.

Only as she did so did she remember that when she had gone to bed, she was wearing only her vest and petticoat.

Outside the Earl pulled her to her feet and then he put a black *burnous* over her shoulders. It was what the Arabs always wore.

Although she could see him only dimly she realised he was wearing a *burnous* too and the effect was to make them almost invisible against the black tents which surrounded them.

Taking her by the hand he started to move slowly but determinedly along the side of the tents.

Vanda remembered being told that the Sheik's tent was always on the West side of the camp and facing West. The most important guest, or in her case his prisoner, occupied a tent directly behind it.

At the moment the camp was quiet.

Vanda guessed that all the Arabs were in front of the other side of the camp, waiting for the attack they expected from Sheik Abu's tribesmen.

The Earl walked on ahead quickly and now he was moving even faster. It seemed to Vanda a very long way, although there were still tents on one side of them and when they came to a small group of trees, the Earl turned in amongst them.

Now it was painful to walk barefooted on the twigs and small fir cones which lay on the ground. Vanda did not say anything but she stumbled and the Earl stopped and picked her up tenderly. He carried her as he had the night when they had dined with Sheik Abu.

She felt a thrill pass through her because she was in his arms. She looked up at him, wishing and almost praying that he would kiss her again.

Then she noticed that just ahead of them there were horses – three horses.

Only when the man in charge of the horses bent forward to kiss her cheek did she realise it was Charles.

She knew however that she must not say a word. The Earl without setting her down on the ground lifted her onto the saddle and mounted the other horse.

They moved slowly and very quietly away through the trees and as they emerged into the desert they started to gallop.

There was enough light from the stars overhead and the moon for Vanda to see clearly and as she glanced back she could see the mass of black tents below them.

She realised the desert over which they were riding was more hilly than she had encountered and they were heading North.

She realised that the plan was to ride well away from the tribesmen who were watching for the advance of Sheik Abu's men.

She wondered if the Earl and Charles were taking her straight back to the yacht, but when they were completely out of sight of the back tents they turned to go downhill.

They rode round in what Vanda realised was almost a complete circle in order to return to Sheik Abu's house.

It took quite a long time, even though the horse she was riding was as swift as the one she had ridden in the afternoon, but it was sad to think that she had left her white mare behind.

She only hoped they would be kind to her. If they could not keep her as their prize, at least the mare was a prisoner they would appreciate.

An hour and a half later and they had been riding at

full speed all the time, Vanda saw Sheik Abu's house just ahead of her.

It was then that at last she spoke.

The words came from the very depths of her heart,

"You saved me! *You – saved me*! How could – you have been – so brave?"

As she spoke the Earl turned to look at her and she thought how handsome he looked in the moonlight.

"Are you all right?" he asked anxiously. "No one has hurt you?"

"No, but I was very frightened that there would be a battle and tribesmen and horses would be killed or wounded."

"I think we may have avoided that catastrophe," the Earl answered with a deep sigh.

"I never thought we would be able to rescue you," Charles added emotionally.

Vanda did not answer as at that moment they arrived at the back of the house, where it would be impossible for anyone to see them.

As they dismounted servants appeared to take the horses.

Sheik Abu was standing in the open doorway.

"You have brought her back, my Lord," he declared in a voice which showed he was much moved. "How is it possible you could be so daring?"

"The Earl has saved me," Vanda said, "and no one will have the slightest idea until daybreak that I have been rescued."

"Now listen!" the Earl intervened in an authoritative tone. "This is important and must be done at once. To save Your Highness's name we need to leave immediately for Beirut."

They all looked at him in surprise as he continued,

"I want you, Vanda, to dress in your best clothes and for Your Highness to command your men to escort us with their lances, flags and anything else which would appear impressive."

Sheik Abu was listening in astonishment.

He managed to say,

"I do not understand, my Lord."

"What Your Highness is going to do," the Earl resumed, "is to make a dramatic entrance into Beirut. By the time we arrive it will be morning and the streets will be filled with people."

Vanda observed a flash of excitement in the Sheik's eyes.

"You will escort us to the best hotel and host a farewell party for Her Royal Highness for your friends and anyone else who pushes their way in."

"In that case there will be a crowd," Charles interposed somewhat mockingly.

"That is exactly what we want to achieve and when we finally board my yacht, it will be with the band playing and people throwing flowers towards Her Royal Highness which of course Your Highness will have to pay for."

The Sheik gave a little laugh.

"After that, if Sheik Shalaan dares to claim he had successfully taken Her Royal Highness prisoner, everyone will laugh and no one will believe him."

"You are so right!" the Sheik exclaimed. "The plan is brilliant and only your Lordship could think of anything so splendid."

"Then hurry and let us start as quickly as possible," the Earl urged, "just in case the Hassein tribesmen decide to sneak up on us as we have not attacked them."

Sheik Abu saw the sense of the Earl's plan of action and started giving orders to the servants who were standing behind him.

Vanda ran to her room where she found Carstairs and he had packed all her trunks.

"You're back!" he exclaimed as she appeared. "I knows as his Lordship would've done it if no one else could."

"He was wonderful," Vanda sighed. "I thought it would be impossible for me to be freed without a battle and a great many people being killed."

"I thinks the same," Carstairs replied. "I've left your blue riding habit out for you as I expects your pink 'un was left behind."

Vanda suddenly realised that her *burnous* was open at the front and Carstairs could see her petticoat.

"That is true," she said, "but I will soon dress in what you have left for me."

"I'll wake one of them women."

He was gone before Vanda could say that she could manage on her own.

The two women who had obviously been asleep came hurrying in rubbing their eyes and they were delighted to see Vanda. They started to say how worried they had been when they heard the news that she had been kidnapped.

However she told them she must hurry and not talk. They waited while she washed as well as she could before helping her into her riding clothes.

She was really very quick.

When she hurried back to find the men, they were waiting outside the front door with the new horse she was to ride.

Sheik Abu was already mounted on a magnificent black stallion.

He was talking to Charles and it was therefore the Earl who picked Vanda up and set her on the saddle.

As he touched her she felt the same thrill running through her.

As he stayed for a moment arranging the skirt of her habit she told him softly,

"Thank you, thank you. You know how grateful I am."

"We will talk about it all later. We are, as you know, still in danger until I can move the Sheik and his men well away from here."

"You – are so – wonderful," Vanda whispered.

As he was mounting his horse she was not certain if he had heard her.

Sheik Abu set off riding in front to lead the way with Vanda just behind him and the Earl and Charles on either side of her.

Behind came the Sheik's personal bodyguard followed by a huge contingent of the warriors of his tribe. Vanda understood with a little shudder that they were the men who had been prepared to go into battle over her.

Quite a number of the small tribes had remained overnight and had no intention of missing the fun, so they followed the cavalcade in front of them.

It was only about four o'clock in the morning and the moon was still at its height and there was no need to travel very fast.

Vanda remembered it had taken them what had seemed a long time to ride from Beirut to the Sheik's house, but she reckoned that they should arrive in Beirut somewhere about eight o'clock. Then, as the Earl had said, the streets would be full with people doing their shopping.

She glanced at him riding beside her and was thinking how marvellously dashing he had been to rescue her from the clutches of Sheik Abu's sworn enemy.

If he had been caught he too would have been a prisoner and perhaps he would not have been treated as well as she had been.

She wanted him to tell her what he had felt when she was reported missing, but it was however difficult to talk when they were just behind the Sheik.

The dawn came swiftly and the sun rose steadily in the sky.

Just as the Earl had anticipated the City of Beirut had come alive and the streets were filled with people hurrying to and fro. The children were either going to school or playing games with each other.

Then as the Sheik appeared looking magnificent in his robes and wearing his most impressive turban, everyone stopped to stare. Behind them the tribesmen were waving their lances and flags with great enthusiasm.

The children were very excited by the procession and ran behind the horses as they moved slowly through the twisting streets towards the centre of the City.

They rode, as Vanda expected, to the same hotel where they had been taken on the day they arrived.

Just before they had left the Sheik's house, Vanda heard that a messenger had been sent ahead and he had obviously alerted the hotel as the manager and staff were waiting for them on the doorstep.

They bowed subserviently to the Sheik and to Vanda and they were shown into the large dining room where servants were hurrying backwards and forwards with plates of sweetmeats and drinks.

"I expect you would like to titivate yourself," Charles suggested teasing her.

Vanda gave a little giggle before she followed a woman who took her to one of the bedrooms.

When she looked at herself in the mirror she felt she was in considerable need of 'titivating' as the ride, although they had not been hurrying, had left her dusty and dishevelled. Her face, she thought, needed washing and so did her hands.

She did not feel tired at all, only elated with excitement. She was not only safe but she was going home with the Earl!

'When we are on the yacht I shall at last be able to talk to him,' she told herself.

She was really hoping that he would kiss her again and it would be the most wonderful dream that could ever come true.

'I love him. I love him with all my heart and soul,' she repeated to herself over and over again.

She looked in the mirror again and wondered if she was pretty enough for him.

There must be so many women in his life.

Perhaps after all he had only kissed her because he did not want her to cry out at the sight of him.

'I love him. I love him,' she whispered once more.

Then she returned to where the Sheik was receiving his guests. The big room was already nearly full.

Vanda was introduced to a number of men and next the Earl suggested that they should all sit down. This was the signal for the servants to bring in the food, which was a combination of breakfast, luncheon, and the Bedouins' favourite dishes.

The Earl prompted Sheik Abu into making a speech.

As he spoke in Arabic it was difficult to follow everything he was saying, but Vanda was conscious that he was being very complimentary to her.

She therefore smiled and tried to look a little embarrassed as if his compliments were overwhelming.

More and more tribesmen kept arriving until the room was packed to bursting.

Finally the Earl announced that it was time for them to go aboard the yacht.

Vanda had calculated that by now their luggage would have arrived and been taken to the *Sea Serpent* and she agreed that it would be a mistake to outstay their welcome.

There was a carriage waiting outside the hotel to convey them and Sheik Abu to the port with most of the party following on horseback, in carriages or on foot.

Once again it was a magnificent procession through the streets of the City. Whether or not the populace realised who was passing them in such state, the women waved and the children cheered.

As the Earl had suggested a band appeared from nowhere and was playing on the quay as they arrived.

The Earl's yacht had been dressed with flags and bunting and when the carriage ground to a standstill, the Captain greeted them.

They were piped aboard.

The Earl had decreed that only the Sheik should actually come on board the *Sea Serpent*, whilst the tribesmen gathered on the quay.

"We have so much to thank Your Highness for," the Earl began.

"On the contrary, my Lord," Sheik Abu replied. "I must thank you from the bottom of my heart for all your help and assistance."

They knew what he meant and there was a little pause before he added,

"The horses, I promise you, will be despatched tomorrow or at the latest by the end of the week!"

It was with difficulty that Vanda did not give a shout of joy.

They had won! They had gained the horses they had come for.

She was sure from the way the Sheik spoke that they were not going to have to pay for them and the Earl realised this too.

"Your Highness is extremely generous," he said, "and I can only hope that when you come to England, we can repay your superb hospitality as you have entertained and welcomed us."

"I shall certainly consider making the journey," the Sheik replied.

He shook hands with everyone including the Captain and then he walked slowly down the gangway with the band still playing.

As the gangway was pulled in, the engines began to turn.

A great number of women who had been standing on the quay now rushed forward with flowers and threw them onto the deck of the *Sea Serpent*.

Vanda picked up some of the first flowers which reached her and held them in her arms as if they were a bouquet.

Then as she waved, the crowd waved back and shouted out,

"Allah protect you. *Bon Voyage*. Good Luck."

The air seemed to ring with the words.

Gradually they moved out into the sea and the Sheik stood to attention on the quay until they were nearly out of sight.

It was then that Vanda gave a deep sigh.

"We have done it!" she cried. "And the horses will follow. How could we have been so lucky?"

"All that matters is that you are safe," the Earl murmured in a deep voice.

"That was thanks to you," Charles said. "All I can say, Favin, is that you should be awarded a medal for gallantry."

Vanda gave a little cry,

"That reminds me, your beautiful brooch was pinned on my riding jacket which I left behind. I am sorry, so very sorry, you should lose it."

"Perhaps it will be some compensation for the Sheik we outwitted," the Earl mused. "That we have turned the tables on him will, I promise you, upset him far more than losing you."

Vanda did not say anything.

She was hoping that Sheik Shalaan would one day find someone he could love, just as she loved the Earl.

Because she wanted to take off her hat and change out of her riding clothes, she descended to her cabin.

The Earl went to his writing-desk where he sat down and drew a letter out of his pocket which had been waiting for him.

It was from Mr. Wilson.

He was sure before he opened it that it contained bad news and he could only hope that Irene had not been making more scenes.

He opened the letter and stiffened as he read,

'*My Lord,*

I regret that it is my duty to inform you that His Grace died yesterday.

It was in his sleep and he did not suffer.

After I had placed the announcement in the newspaper, I corresponded immediately with Lord Arthur and explained to him where you were.

He said that you were not to worry as he would see to everything and after your father's long illness, the family would prefer his funeral to be as quiet as possible.'

The letter continued to mention a number of relatives who had called at Brackenshaw House to see if the Earl was in residence.

And then he finished,

'I must also inform Your Lordship that, having heard the news, Lady Grantham came to see me and made a terrible scene about not being able to get in touch with you.

She had expected an answer to her last letter to you and behaved in such an extraordinary manner that I cannot help feeling that she is somewhat deranged.

I am obliged because of her insistence to forward on to you another letter from her.

I only wish I could send your Lordship better news. However everything else, including matters in the country, is exactly as you would wish.

I remain,

Yours respectfully,

Basil Wilson'

The Earl read it through again carefully and then without reading Irene's letter, he tore it up.

He threw the pieces out of the porthole.

He knew only too well that now he had come into his father's title, she would be more determined than ever to marry him.

'What am I to do?' he asked himself. What the devil am I to do?'

He realised now that he loved Vanda in a different way

from anything he had ever felt for any other woman.

He had been amused, enthralled and excited by women like Irene, but they never touched his heart.

He had never contemplated spending any more than a short time with them and he knew now that he wanted to spend the rest of his life with Vanda.

To teach her about love would be the most exciting and wonderful thing he would ever been able to do.

But there was so much more to his love for Vanda.

He felt already as if she was a part of him.

He knew she would do everything he wanted as his wife and as a Duchess.

But – the word seemed to stand out in front of him in letters of fire – Irene would scream and berate him for leaving her. She had already threatened to kill any woman who aroused his interest.

He had an uncomfortable feeling that Irene would be more dangerous than even Sheik Shalaan could have been, as apart from harming Vanda physically, everything she might say or do would besmirch her innocence and purity.

The Earl could not bear to think of it.

'*What can I do*?' he howled at himself again.

He looked out of the open porthole at the sky and thought only God could help him now.

*

Vanda was worried for the rest of the day, while the yacht was moving swiftly through calm waters. She could not understand why it seemed impossible for her to be alone with the Earl.

When she waited for him on deck or in the Saloon, he did not appear if she was alone.

He always seemed to wait until Charles was there first

and she was forced into acknowledging that he was trying to avoid her.

'Why? Why?' she asked herself. 'What – have I – done?'

Every time she saw him she felt her love rising within her like a flood tide and it moved up through her breasts into her lips.

She longed for his kisses.

She craved the ecstasy she had felt when she awoke to find her dream a reality.

'I – love – him,' she murmured as she walked round the deck alone.

She guessed that he was on the bridge with the Captain, so there was no point in joining him there.

At mealtimes he was always laughing and talked mostly with Charles and inevitably they talked about the horses and what they would do with them when they arrived home.

"How could we be so lucky?" Charles asked a dozen times. "We never expected to acquire so many and not to have to pay for them."

"We must thank Vanda for that," the Earl added, "or perhaps to be honest we should also thank Sheik Shalaan!"

"I only wish we could have seen his face," Charles said, "when he walked into her tent and found that she had gone."

"You are not to be too unkind about him," Vanda intervened. "I thought it was sad that he had never really loved anyone in his life and that is just what I believe he really wants."

"Did you talk to him about love?" Charles enquired.

"Yes, I did and I told him that one day he would find the other half of himself and then he would be happy."

"Did he think it would be you?" the Earl wanted to know.

Vanda thought she detected a note in his voice which showed he cared.

"He did suggest it," she replied, "but I told him he would be happier with a Bedouin woman, just as I wanted to marry an Englishman."

Once Vanda had finished speaking, she suddenly felt embarrassed in case the Earl might think she was trying to force his hand to make her a proposal.

"Let us talk some more about the horses," she said quickly. "How many are Charles and I to have and how many are you keeping?"

The Earl hesitated,

"May I give you the answer to that question tomorrow?"

"Why are you being so mysterious?" Charles asked.

"I have a great deal to think about and quite frankly I am finding it difficult after the agitation of our last day in Syria."

Charles laughed.

"I don't blame you, I feel the same. I would like to point out that as we did not sleep a wink last night, I am definitely going to bed now."

"That is exactly what I will do too," Vanda said.

She walked to her own cabin and Carstairs came in to see if there was anything that she required.

He arranged her bath and then she climbed into bed and as she lay her head onto the pillow she realised how very tired she was.

At the same time she was still worrying over the Earl.

"I love – you. *I love – you*," she whispered. "Please, God, let him – love me a – little bit."

The Earl awoke and realised it was already eight o'clock in the morning and that he had been more exhausted than he thought.

He had slept all night, missing dinner, until it was breakfast time.

He was to learn later that Vanda and Charles had done the same.

The sun was streaming in through the portholes and although it seemed to make everything seem bright and happy, the darkness of Irene was still torturing his mind.

Once again the same question seemed to dance in front of his eyes.

'What shall I do? What *shall* I do?'

The door of the cabin opened stealthily and Carstairs peeped in.

"I thinks you'd be awake by now, my Lord and we are now moored alongside at Piraeus."

"I know I have slept the clock round," the Earl replied. "I will get up now and go ashore."

"I've already been ashore, my Lord, and I thinks you'd like to see this."

He said it in such a meaningful way that the Earl gave Carstairs a sharp glance as he handed him a copy of *The Times* of two days ago.

"They hadn't got anything later," Carstairs told him, "but I thinks what you'll find inside be what your Lordship would like to hear."

He left the cabin after he had spoken.

The Earl opened *The Times*, supposing that Carstairs was referring to his father's funeral in a somewhat strange manner.

Then as he read the headlines on the second page, he stiffened.

'TRAGEDY ON ANCESTRAL TOWER

A tragedy occurred yesterday at the ancestral home of Lord Grantham, when both his Lordship and his wife fell from the battlements of the ancient castle which has been in Lord Grantham's family for two centuries.'

There then followed a description of Lord Grantham's distinguished political career.

The Earl read on,

'It is thought that Lord Grantham, who was sometimes unsteady on his legs, had climbed up to the tower as he did occasionally to look at the view.

It is believed that he slipped on the lead of the roof and Lady Grantham, the famous beauty, tried to save her husband from falling.

Unfortunately she was unable to do so and in the struggle to save her husband, she lost her own life as she fell with him. When they hit the ground both Lord and Lady Grantham were killed instantly.

Their bodies were taken to their private Chapel where they will lie in state until the funeral which will take place in a few days time.'

The Earl read the end of the report twice.

He knew exactly what must have really happened, but he did not wish to think about it as there was nothing he could do.

What he thought secretly must never be repeated to anyone.

Above all he was now free.

Free to tell Vanda that he loved her without being afraid or restricted in any way.

He dressed himself quickly without sending for

Carstairs and ran from his cabin and quietly opened the door of Vanda's room.

The curtains were still drawn, but the sunlight was filtering through on either side.

She was in bed and still asleep.

The Earl moved closer to her.

Her golden hair was falling over her shoulders and her left hand with her long beautiful fingers lay limply on the sheet.

He thought no one could look lovelier or more desirable.

Gently he sat down on the bed and bending forward kissed her.

It was a very soft and tender kiss.

Then as her lips responded to his, her arms curled around his neck.

He continued kissing her but now more possessively as if he was afraid of losing her.

He raised his head.

"I – love – you," Vanda muttered sleepily. "*I – love – you.*"

"And I love you, my darling," the Earl whispered.

She opened her eyes.

"Are – you – really – here?"

"Really and truly," the Earl answered. "You must wake up because we have so much to do."

"I – just want – you to go on – kissing – me," she murmured.

"That is just what I want too," he breathed passionately, "but I think perhaps we had better be married first."

His words made Vanda open her eyes wide.

"Married!" she exclaimed.

"We are going to be married here in Athens at the British Embassy Church," the Earl announced. "Then I know you want to go to Delphi. You told me so long ago."

"I cannot believe – what you are – saying," Vanda sighed. "Do you – really and truly – want me – as your – wife?"

"I want you more than I have ever wanted anything in the whole of my life. I love you, my darling, as I will swear before God when we are in the Church, and I will do everything in my power to make you happy."

"I *am* happy, so wildly – happy," Vanda cried. "I thought – you had only – kissed me to keep me from – crying out in the tent and did not – really mean it."

"I will show you how much I mean it and how wonderful it will be for both of us when we are married."

"Then let – us be married – quickly, in case – we wake up and – find that this – is just a wonderful – dream."

"We will dream together and we will never wake up," the Earl said firmly. "God has looked after us and made us luckier than I ever thought possible."

He knew as he spoke the words that it was the truth.

He really had been so lucky, in fact the luckiest man in the world.

Not only to have found Vanda but to lose Irene.

He was grateful, so grateful that he could only say to Vanda again,

"I promise I will make you happy, my precious darling, and we will make everyone we know happy with us."

*

There were no difficulties for the Duke of Brackenshaw to be married immediately in the British

Embassy Church in Athens.

The Ambassador and his wife considered it all very delightful.

The Earl told them that his future wife did not have a veil with her and the Ambassador's wife produced one and a very pretty diamond tiara.

He thought that no bride could have looked more gorgeous.

They drove to the Church accompanied by Charles, who was to give Vanda away.

Before they left the yacht the Captain, the Chief Steward and their wives were let into the secret of why Vanda had been pretending to be a Princess.

They all thought the story most intriguing. In fact so much so that the Duke only hoped they would keep their promise of not repeating it to anyone.

"Do you really think, Your Grace," the Captain asked, "that the horses will follow you back to England?"

"I am convinced that the Sheik was so grateful to us that we will not be disappointed," the Earl replied.

When he drove away from the yacht with Vanda and Charles, he left behind a large number of instructions.

*

The service in the British Embassy Church was simple but, Vanda thought, very moving.

The Chaplain conducted the service with great sincerity and when he blessed the bride and groom, she felt as though they had been doubly blessed.

It was as if God had taken them especially under His protection.

In the future they would always be safe.

As they drove back to the yacht Charles told them he

143

had made arrangements with the Ambassador to return by train.

"I have always wanted to travel on the Orient Express," he explained, "and this is my very best opportunity. I will also have a great deal to do at home when the horses arrive. What arrangements am I to make for you, Favin?"

"You are to take them all and start training them for the Racecourse."

"All of them!" Charles queried in astonishment.

"All except two, which we will change over from time to time for Vanda and me to ride. We are to be a partnership in the future and you are to undertake all the training."

"A partnership!"

"It is what Vanda would like more than anything and so should I. We will join our colours and race our horses together and if we do not win all the Classics I shall be very surprised!"

Charles was for the moment overwhelmed.

"I cannot believe it," he said.

"You are doing me a favour as well as yourself," the Earl said. "Now that I have all my father's affairs to organise, there is a great deal to be done and Vanda and I will have to work very hard to bring the estate up to modern standards. Therefore we will leave the horses happily in your care."

Vanda slipped her hand into his.

He knew how much his suggestion pleased her and how grateful she was.

"Thirty Arab horses!" he sighed.

"Twenty-eight," the Earl corrected him. "And do not forget we shall want only the best. When you change them over, we will take the best again before the races begin."

Charles grinned,

"I can see there are going to be endless arguments over this arrangement."

"It is such a wonderful idea!" Vanda joined in, "and thank you, thank you, my wonderful husband, for being so kind and generous to Charles and me."

She said these words in a soft caressing voice and the Earl thought it was like listening to music.

He felt that his wife looked far more beautiful than any Greek Goddess could ever have been and he knew that his life in the future was going to be very different from anything he had experienced in the past.

In Vanda's own words – '*wonderful*'.

When they reached the *Sea Serpent* it was to find that it was covered in flowers of all colours and fragrance.

Carstairs and the Steward had somehow managed to produce a wedding cake and it was displayed proudly on the table in the Saloon.

There was champagne for everyone, including the crew.

Charles bade the newly-weds an emotional farewell.

"Do enjoy a magnificent honeymoon," he wished them as he hugged Vanda and warmly shook the Earl's hand.

"We have every intention of doing so," Vanda promised. "And we shall be thinking of you surrounded by all those glorious Arab horses."

She waved to Charles from the deck of the *Sea Serpent* as he drove away with his luggage.

Then her husband drew her away.

"I want you to come and look at our cabin."

Vanda wondered why, but did not ask any questions.

The Earl took her to the Master cabin where he had

always slept and when he opened the door, Vanda saw that the whole cabin was decorated entirely in white flowers.

She knew again that it was Carstairs who had managed it, yet undoubtedly her wonderful husband had thought of the idea.

There were white roses and lilies.

The whole room looked like a bower.

"Thank you, my dearest husband," Vanda sighed. "Now I really feel like a bride."

As she spoke she felt the engines begin to turn under her feet.

"Where are we going?" she asked before giving a little cry. "I know it is to Delphi! But I did not think we would go so soon."

"Where else could I take a Goddess?" the Earl asked in a deep voice.

He lifted her tiara and veil as he spoke and kissed her lips, her nose and her eyes.

"The Greeks," he told her quietly, "were the only people who really understood love. The love which you and I, my darling, are going to teach each other and which will be as new and exciting to me as it is to you."

"Oh, Favin, I love you so very much," Vanda murmured with happiness. "You fill my whole world and there is no one in my life but you."

"That is just what I want you to think," the Earl answered as his lips found hers yet again.

*

Sometime later Vanda stirred against her husband's shoulder.

"How can love be so wonderful and so perfect?" she sighed. "Oh, darling Favin, please never stop loving me."

"I have only just started and we both of us have so much to learn from each other."

"I know how ignorant I am. But there have been many lovely ladies in your life?"

"I am not denying it and I have never loved anyone as I love you. I really believe that I worship you, because you are everything I have looked for and thought I would never find."

"Is that really the truth?"

"I swear it is, my precious," the Earl vowed. "We are going to cherish our lives and love will grow within us day by day and year by year. We must never spoil love and we must never lose it."

He spoke so seriously and with such sincerity that Vanda felt moved.

"I am – only afraid," she whispered in a small voice, "of disappointing – you and that you will – find me dull after all – those other beautiful – women."

The Earl drew in his breath.

What he felt for Vanda was completely different from anything he had ever felt in his entire life.

He could not explain his feelings to anyone except himself.

To him she was something holy and very precious and had come to him from Heaven.

It had nothing to do with anything in the past he had vaguely thought was love.

What they had between them now was the love of God.

The love which was the whole basis of living.

The love which raised a man and a woman from being just human to something Divine.

It was impossible for anyone to explain in words.

As he drew Vanda closer into his arms he knew he had found in her the mystery of the Holy Grail which all men seek but few are privileged to find.

It was something he could never lose.

It would make them both supremely happy in themselves.

It would also enable them to give happiness to their children, their grandchildren and all those with whom they ever came into contact.

This was love, the real Love.

The love which passeth all understanding and which comes from God and only God.